• G I F T S •

Ursula Le Guin

Orion

The right of Ursula Le Guin to be identified as the
author of this work has been asserted by her in accordance
with the Copyright, Designs and Patents Act 1988.

First published in the United States of America
in 2004 by Harcourt, Inc.

First published in the United Kingdom in 2004 by
Orion Children's Books
Paperback edition published 2005
by Orion Children's Books
A division of the Orion Publishing Group
Orion House, 5 Upper St Martin's Lane,
London WC2H 9EA

A CIP catalogue record for this book
is available from the British Library

ISBN 1 84255 498 0

Printed in Great Britain by Clays Ltd, St Ives plc

www.orionbooks.co.uk

◆ GIFTS ◆

❖ 1 ❖

He was lost when he came to us, and I fear the silver spoons he stole from us didn't save him when he ran away and went up into the high domains. Yet in the end the lost man, the runaway man, was our guide.

Gry called him the runaway man. When he first came, she was sure he'd done some terrible thing, a murder or a betrayal, and was escaping vengeance. What else would bring a Lowlander here, among us?

"Ignorance," I said. "He knows nothing of us. He's not afraid of us."

"He said people down there warned him not to come up among the witches."

"But he knows nothing about the gifts," I said. "It's all just talk, to him. Legends, lies…"

We were both right, no doubt. Certainly Emmon was running away, if only from a well-earned reputation for thievery, or from boredom; he was as restless, as fearless and inquisitive and inconsequential as a hound puppy, trotting wherever his nose led him. Recalling the accent and turns of speech he had, I know now that he came from far in the south, farther than Algalanda, where tales of the Uplands were just that—tales: old rumors of the distant northland, where wicked witch-folk lived in icy mountains and did impossible things.

If he'd believed what they told him down in Danner, he'd never have come up to Caspromant. If he'd believed us, he never would have gone on higher in the mountains. He loved to hear stories, so he listened to ours, but he didn't believe them. He was a city man, he'd had some education, he'd travelled the length of the Lowlands. He knew the world. Who were we, me and Gry? What did we know, a blind boy and a grim girl, sixteen years old, stuck in the superstition and squalor of the desolate hill farms that we so grandly called our domains? He led us on, in his lazy kindness, to talk about the great powers we had, but while we talked he was seeing the bare, hard way we lived, the cruel poverty, the cripples and backward people of the farms, seeing our ignorance of everything outside these dark hills, and saying to himself, Oh yes, what great powers they have, poor brats!

Gry and I feared that when he left us he went to Geremant. It is hard to think he may still be there, alive but a slave, with legs twisted like corkscrews, or his face made monstrous for Erroy's amusement, or his eyes truly blinded, as mine were not. For Erroy wouldn't have suffered his careless airs, his insolence, for an hour.

I took some pains to keep him away from my father when his tongue was flapping, but only because Canoc's patience was short and his mood dark, not because I feared he'd ever use his gift without good cause. In any case he paid little heed to Emmon or anyone else. Since my mother's death his mind was all given to grief and rage and rancor. He huddled over his pain, his longing for vengeance. Gry, who knew all the nests and eyries for miles around, once saw a carrion eagle brooding his pair of silvery, grotesque eaglets in a nest up on the Sheer, after a shepherd killed the mother bird who hunted for them both. So my father brooded and starved.

To Gry and me, Emmon was a treasure, a bright creature come into our gloom. He fed our hunger. For we were starving too.

He would never tell us enough about the Lowlands. He'd give an answer of some kind to every question I asked, but often a joking answer, evasive or merely vague. There was probably a good deal about his past life that he didn't want us to know, and anyhow he wasn't a keen observer and clear reporter, as Gry was when she was my eyes. She could describe exactly how the new bull calf looked, his bluish coat and knobby legs and little furry hornbuds, so that I could all but see him. But if I asked Emmon to tell about the city of Derris Water, all he said was that it wasn't much of a city and the market was dull. Yet I knew, because my mother had told me, that Derris Water had tall red houses and deep streets, that steps of slate led up from the docks and moorages where the river traffic came and went, that there was a market of birds, and a market of fish, and a market of spices and incense and honey, a market for old clothes and a market for new ones, and the great pottery fairs to which people came from all up and down the Trond River, even from the far shores of the ocean.

Maybe Emmon had had bad luck with his thieving in Derris Water.

Whatever the reason, he preferred to ask us the questions and sit back at ease to listen to us—to me, mostly. I was always a talker, if there was anybody to listen. Gry had a long habit of silence and watchfulness, but Emmon could draw her out.

I doubt he knew how lucky he'd been in finding us two, but he appreciated our making him welcome and keeping him comfortable through a bitter, rainy winter. He was sorry for us. He was bored, no doubt. He was inquisitive.

"So what is it this fellow up at Geremant does that's so fearsome?" he'd ask, his tone just skeptical enough that I'd try as hard as I could to convince him of the truth of what I said. But these were matters that were not much talked about, even among people with the gift. It seemed unnatural to speak of them aloud.

"The gift of that lineage is called the twisting," I said at last.

"Twisting? Like a sort of dancing?"

"No." The words were hard to find, and hard to say. "Twisting people."

"Making them turn around?"

"No. Their arms, legs. Necks. Bodies." I twisted my own body a bit with discomfort at the subject. Finally I said, "You saw old Gonnen, that woodsman, up over Knob Hill. We passed him yesterday on the cart road. Gry told you who he was."

"All bent over like a nutcracker."

"Brantor Erroy did that to him."

"Doubled him up like that? What for?"

"A punishment. The brantor said he came on him picking up wood in Gere Forest."

After a little, Emmon said, "Rheumatism will do that to a man."

"Gonnen was a young man then."

"So you don't yourself recall it happening."

"No," I said, vexed by his airy incredulity. "But he does. And my father does. Gonnen told him. Gonnen said he wasn't in Geremant at all, but only near the borderline, in our woods. Brantor Erroy saw him and shouted, and Gonnen was scared, and started to run away with the load of wood on his back. He fell. When he tried to stand, his back was bent over and hunched, the way it is now. If he tries to stand up, his wife said, he screams with the pain."

"And how did the brantor do this to him?"

Emmon had learned the word from us; he said he'd never heard it in the Lowlands. A brantor is the master or mistress of a domain, which is to say the chief and most gifted of a lineage. My father was Brantor of Caspromant. Gry's mother was Brantor of the Barres of Roddmant and her father Brantor of the Rodds of that domain. We two were their heirs, their nestling eaglets.

I hesitated to answer Emmon's question. His tone had not been mocking, but I didn't know if I should say anything at all about the powers of the gift.

Gry answered him. "He'd have looked at the man," she said in her quiet voice. In my blindness her voice always brought to me a sense of light air moving in the leaves of a tree. "And pointed his left hand or finger at him, and maybe said his name. And then he'd have said a word, or two, or more. And it was done."

"What kind of words?"

Gry was silent; maybe she shrugged. "The Gere gift's not mine," she said at last. "We don't know its ways."

"Ways?"

"The way a gift acts."

"Well, how does your gift act, what does it do, then?" Emmon asked her, not teasing, alive with curiosity. "It's something to do with hunting?"

"The Barre gift is calling," Gry said.

"Calling? What do you call?"

"Animals."

"Deer?" After each question came a little silence, long enough for a nod. I imagined Gry's face, intent yet closed, as she nodded. "Hares?— Wild swine?— Bear?— Well, if you called a bear and it came to you, what would you do then?"

"The huntsmen would kill it." She paused, and said, "I don't call to the hunt."

Her voice was not wind in leaves as she said it, but wind on stone.

Our friend certainly didn't understand what she meant, but her tone may have chilled him a little. He didn't go on with her, but turned to me. "And you, Orrec, your gift is—?"

"The same as my father's," I said. "The Caspro gift is called the undoing. And I will not tell you anything about it, Emmon. Forgive me."

"It's you must forgive my clumsiness, Orrec," Emmon said after a little silence of surprise, and his voice was so warm, with the courtesy and softness of the Lowlands in it, like my mother's voice, that my eyes prickled with tears under the seal that shut them.

He or Gry built up our end of the fire. The warmth of it came round my legs again, very welcome. We were sitting in the big hearth of the Stone House of Caspromant, in the south corner, where seats are built deep into the stones of the chimneyside. It was a cold evening of late January. The wind up in the chimney hooted like great owls. The spinning women were gathered over at the other side of the hearth where the light was better. They talked a little or droned their long, soft, dull spinning songs, and we three in our corner went on talking.

"Well, what about the others, then?" Emmon asked, irrepressible. "You can tell about them, maybe? The other brantors, all over these mountains here, in their stone towers, eh, like this one? on their domains— What powers do they have? What are their gifts? What are they feared for?"

There was always that little challenge of half-disbelief, which I could not resist meeting. "The women of the lineage of Cordemant have the power of blinding," I said, "or making deaf, or taking speech away."

"Well, that's ugly," he said, sounding impressed, for the moment.

"Some of the Cordemant men have the same gift," Gry said.

"Your father, Gry, the Brantor of Roddmant—has he a gift, or is it all your mother's?"

"The Rodds have the gift of the knife," she said.

"And that would be…"

"To send a spellknife into a man's heart or cut his throat with it or kill him or maim him with it how they please, if he's within sight."

"By all the names of all the sons of Chorm, that's a nice trick! A pretty gift! I'm glad you take after your mother."

"So am I," Gry said.

He kept coaxing and I couldn't resist the sense of power it gave me to tell him of the powers of my people. So I told him of the Olm lineage, who can set a fire burning at any place they can see and point to; and the Callems, who can move heavy things by word and gesture, even buildings, even hills; and the Morga lineage, who have the innersight, so that they see what you're thinking—though Gry said what they saw was any illness or weakness that might be in you. We agreed that in either case the Morgas could be uncomfortable neighbors, though not dangerous ones, which is why they keep out of the way, on poor domains far over in the northern glens, and no one knows much about them except that they breed good horses.

Then I told him what I had heard all my life about the lineages of the great domains, Helvarmant, Tibromant, Borremant, the warlords of the Carrantages, up on the mountain to the northeast. The gift of the Helvars was called cleansing, and it was akin to the gift of my lineage, so I said no more about it. The gifts of the Tibros and the Borres were called the rein and the broom. A man of Tibromant could take your will from you and make you do his will; that was the rein. Or a woman of Borremant could take your mind from you and leave you a blank idiot, brainless and speechless; that was the broom. And it was done, as with all such powers, with a glance, a gesture, a word.

But those powers were hearsay to us as much as to Emmon. There were none of those great lineages here in the Uplands, and brantors of the Carrantages did not mix with us people of the low domains, though they raided down the mountain now and then for serfs.

"And you fight back, with your knives and fires and all," Emmon said. "I can see why you live so scattered out!...And the folk on west of here that you've spoken of, the big domain, Drummant, is it? What's their brantor's way of making you unhappy? I like to know these things before I meet a fellow."

I did not speak. "The gift of Brantor Ogge is the slow wasting," Gry said.

Emmon laughed. He could not know not to laugh at that.

"Worst yet!" he said. "Well, I take it back about those people with the innersight, is it, who can tell you what ails you. After all, that could be a useful gift."

"Not against a raid," I said.

"Are you always fighting each other, then, your domains?"

"Of course."

"What for?"

"If you don't fight, you're taken over, your lineage is broken." I treated his ignorance rather loftily. "That's what the gifts are for, the powers—so you can protect your domain and keep your lineage pure. If we couldn't protect ourselves we'd lose the gift. We'd be overrun by other lineages, and by common people, or even by *callucs*—" I stopped short. The word on my lips stopped me, the contemptuous word for Lowlanders, people of no gift, a word I had never said aloud in my life.

My mother had been a calluc. They had called her that at Drummant.

I could hear Emmon poking with a stick in the

ashes, and after a while he said, "So these powers, these gifts, run in the family line, from father to son, like a snub nose might do?"

"And from mother to daughter," said Gry, as I said nothing.

"So you've all got to marry in the family to keep the gift in the family. I can see that. Do the gifts die out if you can't find a cousin to marry?"

"It's not a problem in the Carrantages," I said. "The land's richer up there, the domains are bigger, with more people on them. A brantor there may have a dozen families of his lineage on his domain. Down here, the lineages are small. Gifts get weakened if there are too many marriages out of the lineage. But the strong gift runs true. Mother to daughter, father to son."

"And so your trick with the animals came from your mother, the lady-brantor"—he gave the word a feminine form, which sounded ridiculous—"And Orrec's gift is from Brantor Canoc, and I'll ask no more about that. But you will tell me, now that you know I ask in friendship, were you born blind, Orrec? Or those witches you told of, from Cordemant, did they do this to you, in spite, or a feud, or a raid?"

I did not know how to put his question aside, and had no half-answer for it.

"No," I said. "My father sealed my eyes."

"Your father! Your father blinded you?"

I nodded.

◆ 2 ◆

To see that your life is a story while you're in the middle of living it may be a help to living it well. It's unwise, though, to think you know how it's going to go, or how it's going to end. That's to be known only when it's over.

And even when it's over, even when it's somebody else's life, somebody who lived a hundred years ago, whose story I've heard told time and again, while I'm hearing it I hope and fear as if I didn't know how it would end; and so I live the story and it lives in me. That's as good a way as I know to outwit death. Stories are what death thinks he puts an end to. He can't understand that they end in him, but they don't end with him.

Other people's stories may become part of your own, the foundation of it, the ground it goes on. So it was with my father's story of the Blind Brantor; and his story of the raid on Dunet; and my mother's stories of the Lowlands and of the time when Cumbelo was King.

When I think of my childhood, I enter into the hall of the Stone House, I am in the hearth seat, in the muddy courtyard or the clean stables of Caspromant; I am in the kitchen garden with my mother picking beans, or with her by the hearth in the round tower room; I am out on the open hills with Gry; I am in the world of the never-ending stories.

A great, thick staff of yew wood, crudely cut but polished black at the grip by long use, hung beside the door of the Stone House, in the dark entryway: Blind Caddard's staff. It was not to be touched. It was much taller than I was when I first knew that. I used to go and touch it secretly for the thrill of it, because it was forbidden, because it was a mystery.

I thought Brantor Caddard had been my father's father, for that was as far back in history as my understanding went. I knew my grandfather's name had been Orrec. I was named for him. So, in my mind, my father had two fathers. I had no difficulty with that, but found it interesting.

I was in the stables with my father, looking after the horses. He did not fully trust any of his people with his horses, and had begun training me to help him with them when I was three. I was up on a step stool currying the winter hair out of the roan mare's coat. I asked my father, who was working on the big grey stallion in the next stall, "Why did you only name me for one of your fathers?"

"I had only one to name you for," my father said. "Like most respectable folk." He did not often laugh, but I could see his dry smile.

"Then who was Brantor Caddard?"—but then I had figured it out before he could answer—"He was your father's father!"

"My father's father's father's father," Canoc said, through the cloud of winter fur and dust and dried mud he was bringing up out of Greylag's coat. I kept tugging and whacking and combing away at the mare's flank, and was rewarded with rubbish in my eyes and nose and mouth, and a patch of bright white-and-red spring coat the size of my hand on Roanie's flank, and a rumble of contentment from her. She was like a cat; if you petted her she leaned on you. I pushed her off as hard as I could and worked on, trying to enlarge the bright patch. There were too many fathers for me to keep straight.

The one I had came around to the front of the mare's stall, wiping his face, and stood there watching me. I worked away, showing off, pushing the currycomb now in strokes too long to do much good. But my father didn't say anything about it. He said, "Caddard had the greatest gift of our lineage, or any other of the western hills. The greatest that was ever given us. What is the gift of our lineage, Orrec?"

I stopped work, stepped down from the stool, carefully, because it was a long step down for me, and stood facing my father. When he said my name, I stood up, stood still, and faced him: so I had done as far back as I could remember.

"Our gift is the undoing," I said.

He nodded. He was always gentle with me. I had no fear of harm from him. Obeying him was a difficult, intense pleasure. His satisfaction was my reward.

"What does that mean?"

I said as he had taught me to say: "It means the power to undo, unmake, destroy."

"Have you seen me use that power?"

"I saw you make a bowl go all to pieces."

"Have you seen me use that power on a living thing?"

"I saw you make a willow wand go all soft and black."

I hoped he would stop, but that was no longer where these questions stopped.

"Have you seen me use that power on a living animal?"

"I saw you make...a...make a rat die."

"How did it die?" His voice was quiet and relentless.

It was in the winter. In the courtyard. A trapped rat. A young rat. It had got into a rain barrel and been unable to clamber out. Darre the sweeper saw it first. My father said, "Come here, Orrec," and I came, and he said, "Be still and see this," and I stood still and watched. I craned my neck so that I could see the rat swimming in the water that half-filled the barrel. My father stood above the barrel, gazing down steadily into it. He moved his hand, his left hand, and said something or breathed sharply out. The rat squirmed once, shuddered, and floated on the water. My father reached his right hand in and brought it out. It lay utterly limp in his hand, shapeless, like a wet rag, not like a rat. But

I saw the tail and toes with their tiny claws. "Touch it, Orrec," he said. I touched it. It was soft, without bones, like a little half-filled sack of meal inside its thin wet skin. "It is unmade," my father said, his eyes on mine, and I was afraid of his eyes then.

"You unmade it," I said now, in the stable, with a dry mouth, afraid of my father's eyes.

He nodded.

"I have that power," he said, "as you will. And as it grows in you, I'll teach you the way to use it. What is the way to use your gift?"

"With eye and hand and breath and will," I said, as he had taught me.

He nodded, satisfied. I relaxed a little; but he did not. The test was not over.

"Look at that knot of hair, Orrec," he said. A little clotted tangle of muddy horsehair lay on the stable floor near my feet, among the slight littering of straw. It had been caught in the roan mare's mane, and I had worked it free and let it drop. At first I thought my father was going to scold me for dirtying the stable floor.

"Look at it. At it only. Don't look away from it. Keep your eyes on it."

I obeyed.

"Move your hand—so." Coming behind me, my father moved my left arm and hand gently, carefully, till the joined fingers pointed at the clot of mud and hair. "Hold it so. Now, say what I say after me. With your breath but not your voice. Say this." He whispered something that had no meaning to me, and I whispered it after him, holding my hand pointing as he had placed it, staring and staring at the clot of hair.

For a moment nothing moved, everything held still. Then Roanie sighed and shifted her feet, and I heard the wind gusting outside the stable door, and the tangle of muddy hair on the floor moved a little.

"It moved!" I cried.

"The wind moved it," my father said. His voice was mild, with a smile in it. He stood differently, stretched his shoulders. "Wait a while. You're not six yet."

"You do it, Father," I said, staring at the clot of horsehair, excited and angry, vindictive. "You unmake it!"

I scarcely saw him move or heard his breath. The tangled thing on the floor uncurled in a puff of dust, and nothing lay there but a few long, reddish-cream hairs.

"The power will come to you," Canoc said. "The gift is strong in our lineage. But in Caddard it was strongest. Sit down here. You're old enough to know his story."

I sat perched on the step stool. My father stood in the doorway of the stall, a thin, straight, dark man, bare-legged in his heavy black Uplander kilt and coat, his eyes dark and bright through the mask of stable dirt on his face. His hands were filthy too, but they were strong, fine hands, steady, without restlessness. His voice was quiet. His will was strong.

He told me the story of Blind Caddard.

"Caddard showed his gift earlier than any son of our lineage, or any but the greatest families of the Carrantages. At three, he'd gaze at his toys and they'd fall to pieces, and he could untie a knot with a look. At four, he used his power against a dog that leapt on him and frightened him, and destroyed it. As I destroyed that rat."

He paused for my nod of acknowledgment.

"The servants were afraid of him, and his mother said, 'While his will is a child's will, he is a danger to us all, even to me.' She was a woman of our lineage; she and her husband Orrec were cousins. He heeded her warning. They tied a bandage around the child's eyes for three years, so that he couldn't use the power of the eye. All that time they taught and trained him. As I teach you and train you. He learned well. His reward for perfect obedience was to see again. And he was careful, using his great gift only in practice, on things of no use or value.

"Only twice in his youth did he show his power. Once, when the Brantor of Drummant had been raiding cattle from one domain and another, they invited him to Caspromant and let him see Caddard, who was a boy of twelve then, unmake a flight of wild geese. With one glance and gesture he dropped them from the sky. He did this smilingly, as if to entertain their visitor. 'A keen eye,' Drum said. And he stole none of our cattle.

"Then when Caddard was seventeen a war party came down from the Carrantages led by the Brantor of Tibromant. They were after men and women to work new fields they'd cleared. Our people came running here to the Stone House for protection, fearing to be taken under the rein, made to follow that brantor and die toiling for him with no will but his left to them. Caddard's father Orrec hoped to withstand the raid here in the Stone House, but Caddard, not telling him what he planned, went out alone. Keeping to the edge of the forest, he spied out one highlander and then another, and as he saw them he unmade them."

I saw the rat. The soft sack of skin.

"He let the other highlanders find those bodies. Then carrying the parley flag he came out on the hillside, facing the Long Cairn, alone. He called to the raiders, 'I have done this across a mile of distance, and farther.' He called to them over the valley, as they stood up there behind the great rocks of the Cairn, 'The rocks do not hide you from me.' And he destroyed a standing stone of the Cairn. The Brantor of Tibromant had taken shelter behind it. It shattered and fell into chips and dust. 'My eye is strong,' Caddard said.

"He waited for them to answer. Tibro said, 'Your eye is strong, Caspro.' Caddard said, 'Do you come here seeking servants?' The other said, 'We need men, yes.' Caddard said, 'I will give you two of our people to work for you, but as servants, not under the rein.' The brantor said, 'You are generous. We will take your gift and keep your terms.' Caddard came back here to the house and called out two young serfs from different farms of our domain. He took them to the highlanders and gave them over to them. Then he said to Tibro, 'Go back to your highlands now, and I will not follow.'

"They went, and since that day they have never come raiding from the Carrantages as far west as our domain.

"So Caddard Strong-Eye was the talk of all the Uplands."

He stopped to let me think about what I'd heard. After a while I looked up at him to see if I could ask a question. It seemed to be all right, so I asked what I wanted to know—"Did the young men from our domain want to go to Tibromant?"

"No," my father said. "And Caddard didn't want to send them to serve another master, or lose their labor here. But if power is shown, a gift must be offered. That is important. Remember it. Tell me what I said."

"It's important, if you show your power, to offer a gift too."

My father nodded approval. "The gift's gift," he said, low and dry. "So, then, a while after that, old Orrec went with his wife and some of his people to our high farms, leaving the Stone House to his son Caddard, who was the brantor now. And the domain prospered. We ran a thousand sheep in those days, they say, on the Stony Hills. And our white oxen were famous. Men came up from Dunet and Danner, back then, to bargain for our cattle. Caddard married a woman of the Barres of Drummant, Semedan, in a great wedding. Drum had wanted her for his own son, but Semedan refused him, for all his wealth, and married Caddard. People came to that wedding from all the domains of the west."

Canoc paused. He slapped the roan mare's rump as she switched her snarled tail at him. She shuffled, nudging against me, wanting me to get back to combing the tangles out of her.

"Semedan had the gift of her lineage. She went on the hunt with Caddard and called the deer and elk and wild swine to him. They had a daughter, Assal, and a son, Canoc. And all went well. But after some years there came a bad winter and a cold dry summer, with little grass for the flocks. Crops failed. A plague came among our white cattle. All the finest stock died in a single season. There was sickness among the people of the domain too. Semedan bore a dead child and was ill for a long time after. The drought went on a year, another year. Everything went badly. But Caddard could do nothing. These were not matters in his power. So he lived in rage."

I watched my father's face. Grief, dismay, anger swept over it as he told of them. His bright eyes saw only what he told.

"Our misfortune made the people of Drummant grow insolent, and they came raiding and thieving here. They stole a good horse from our west pastures. Caddard went after the horse thieves and found them halfway home to Drummant. In his heat and fury he did not control his power, but destroyed them all, six men. One of them was a nephew of the Brantor of Drummant. Drum could not ask bloodright, for the men had been thieving, they had the stolen horse with them. But it left a greater hatred between our domains.

"After that, people went in fear of Caddard's temper. When a dog disobeyed him, he unmade it. If he missed his shot hunting, he'd destroy all the thickets that hid the game, leaving them black and ruined. A shepherd spoke some insolence to him, up on the high pastures, and in his anger Caddard withered the man's arm and hand. Children ran from his shadow, now.

"Bad times breed quarrels. Caddard bade his wife come call to the hunt for him. She refused, saying she was not well. He ordered her, 'Come. I must hunt, there is no meat in the house.' She said, 'Go hunt, then. I will not come.' And she turned away, with a serving maid she was fond of, a girl of twelve who helped her with her children. Then in a rage of anger Caddard came in front of them, saying, 'Do what I say!'—and with eye, hand, breath, and will, he struck the girl. She sank down there, destroyed, unmade.

"Semedan cried out and knelt over her and saw she was dead. Then she stood up from the body and faced Caddard. 'Did you not dare strike me?' she said, scorning him. And in his fury, he struck her down.

"The people of the house stood and saw all this. The children cried out and tried to come to their mother, weeping, and the women held them back.

"Then Caddard went out of the hall, to his wife's room, and no one dared follow him.

"When he knew what he had done, he knew what he must do. He could not trust his strength to control his gift. Therefore he blinded his eyes."

The first time Canoc told me that story, he did not say how Caddard blinded himself. I was too young, too scared and bewildered already by this terrible history, to ask or wonder. Later on, when I was older, I asked if Caddard used his dagger. No, Canoc said. He used his gift to undo his gift.

Among Semedan's things was a glass mirror in a silver frame shaped like a leaping salmon. The merchants that used to venture up from Dunet and Danner to bargain for cattle and woollen goods sometimes brought such rare toys and fancies. In the first year of the marriage, Caddard had traded a white bull for the mirror to give to his young wife. He took it in his hand now and looked into it. He saw his own eyes. With hand and breath and will he struck them with the power in them. The glass shattered, and he was blind.

No one sought bloodright against him for the murder of his wife and the girl. Blind as he was, he served as Brantor of Caspromant till he had trained his son Canoc in the use of his power. Then Canoc became brantor and Blind Caddard went up to the high farms, where he lived among the cattle herders till he died.

I did not like all this sad and fearful ending of the story. The first time I heard it, I soon put most of it out of my mind. What I liked was the first part, about the boy with the mighty gift, who could frighten his own mother, and the brave youth defying the enemy and saving his domain. When I went out alone on the open hills, I was Caddard Strong-Eye. A hundred times I summoned the terrified highlanders and called, "I have done this across a mile of distance!"—and shattered the boulder they hid behind, and sent them crawling home. I remembered how my father had held and positioned my left hand, and time and again I stood staring with all my eyes at a rock, and held my hand so, in just that way—but I could not recall the word he had whispered to me, if it had been a word. *With the breath, not the voice*, he had said. I could almost remember it, yet I could not hear the sound of it or feel how my lips and tongue had formed it, if they had formed it. Time and again I almost said it, but said nothing. Then, impatient, I hissed some meaningless sound and pretended that the rock moved, shattered, dropped into dust and fragments, and the highlanders cowered before me as I said, "My eye is strong!"

I would go look at the boulder then, and once or twice I was sure there was a chip or crack in it that had not been there before.

Sometimes when I had been Caddard Strong-Eye long enough, I became one of the farm boys he gave to the highlanders. I escaped from them by clever ruses and woodcraft, and eluded pursuit, and led my pursuers into the bogs I knew and they didn't know, and so came back to Caspromant. Why a serf would want to return to servitude at Caspromant having escaped it at Tibromant I didn't know. I never thought to ask. In all likelihood that is what such a boy would do: he would come home. Our farm people and herders were about as well off as we in the Stone House were. Our fortunes were one. It wasn't fear of our powers that kept them with us, generation after generation. Our powers protected them. What they feared was what they didn't know, what they clung to was what they knew. I knew where I'd go if I were carried off by enemies and escaped. I knew there was nowhere in all the Uplands, or in the broad, bright, lower world my mother told me of, that I would ever love as I loved the bare hills and thin woods, the rocks and bogs of Caspromant. I know it still.

❖ 3 ❖

The other great tale my father told me was of the raid on Dunet, and I liked all of that one, for it had the happiest of endings. It ended, as far as I was concerned, in me.

My father had been a young man in need of a wife. There were people of our lineage at the domains of Corde and Drum. My grandfather had taken pains to keep on good terms with the Cordes and tried to patch over the old ill feeling between Caspros and Drums, not joining forays against them or letting his people do any cattle raiding or sheep stealing from them; this was out of fellowship with his relations at those domains, and because he hoped his son might find a wife among them. Our gift went from father to son, but no one doubted that a mother of the true line strengthened the gift. So, there being no girl of the true line at the home domain, we looked to Cordemant, where there were a number of young men of our family, though only one marriageable woman. She was twenty years older than Canoc. Such a marriage has been made often enough—anything to "keep the gift." But Canoc hesitated, and before Orrec could force the issue, Brantor Ogge of Drummant demanded the woman for his own youngest son. The Cordes were under Ogge's thumb, and gave her to him.

That left only the Caspros of Drummant to furnish a bride within the lineage. There were two girls there who would have done well enough, given a few years more to grow up. They would have been glad to marry back into the domain of their kinfolk. But the old hatred between the Drums and the Caspros was strong in Brantor Ogge. He turned away Orrec's advances, scorned his offers, and married the girls off at fourteen and fifteen, one to a farmer and one to a serf.

This was a deliberate insult to the girls, and to the lineage they came from, and worse yet, a deliberate

weakening of our gift. Few people of the domains ap-
proved of Ogge's arrogance. A fair contest between
powers is one thing, an unfair attack on power itself is
another. But Drummant was a very strong domain, and
Brantor Ogge did as he pleased there.

So there was no woman of the Caspro blood for
Canoc to marry. As he said to me, "Ogge saved me from
the old lady at Cordemant and the poor chicken-faced
girls at Drummant. So I said to my father, 'I'll go
raiding.'"

Orrec thought he meant raiding the small domains
in the Glens, or maybe north into Morgamant, which
had a reputation for fine horses and beautiful women.
But Canoc had a bolder venture in mind. He gathered
a troop, stout young farmers of Caspromant, a couple
of the Caspros of Cordemant, and Ternoc Rodd, and
other young men from one domain or another who
thought a little serf snatching or booty taking was a fine
idea; and they all met one May morning down at the
Crossways under the Sheer and rode down the narrow
track to the south.

There had been no raid into the Lowlands for sev-
enty years.

The farmers wore stiff, thick leather jackets and

bronze caps and carried lance and cudgel and long dagger, in case it came to blood-fighting. The men of the
lineages wore the black felt kilt and coat and went bare-
legged and bare-headed, their long black hair braided
and clubbed. They carried no weapon but a hunting
knife and their eyes.

"When I saw the lot of us, I wished I'd gone first
and stolen some of the Morga horses," Canoc said.
"We'd have been a fine sight but for the creatures most
of us had to ride. I had King"—Roanie's sire, a tall red
horse that I could just remember—"but Ternoc was
on a droop-lipped plowmare, and all Barto had to ride
was a piebald pony with a blind eye. The mules were
handsome, though, three of the fine ones Father bred.
We led them. They were to carry home our loot."

He laughed. He was always light-hearted, telling
this story. I imagine the little procession, the grim,
bright-eyed young men on plodding horses, jingling in
file down the narrow, grassy, rock-strewn track, out of
the Uplands into the world below. Mount Airn would
have risen up behind them when they looked back, and
Barric with its grey crags, and then at last, looming
higher than all, the Carrantages, white-crowned and
huge.

Before them as far as the eye could see lay grassy
hills—"green as beryl," my father said, his eyes looking
back into the memory of that rich, empty land.

On the first day of riding they met no one, saw no
sign of man, no cattle or sheep, only the quail and the
circling hawk. The Lowlanders left a wide margin between themselves and the mountain folk. The raiders
rode all day at the slow pace of Barto's purblind pony
and camped on a hillside. Only late in the morning of
the next day did they begin to see sheep and goats on
stone-fenced hills; then a farmhouse far off, and a mill
down in a stream valley. The track grew to a cart road,
and to a highroad that ran between plowlands, and
then before them, smoke-wreathed and red-roofed on
its sunny hillside, stood the town of Dunet.

I do not know what my father intended his raid to
be—a sudden, fierce onslaught of warriors falling on
terrified townsfolk, or an impressive entry and demands
enforced by the threat of dreaded and uncanny powers.
Whatever he had imagined doing, when he came there
he led his troop to the city and into the streets not at a
gallop, shouting and brandishing weapons, but sedately,
in order. So they went all but unnoticed among the
crowds and flocks and wagons and horse herds of a

market day, until they were right in the central square and marketplace, where suddenly people saw them and began to scream, "Uplanders! Witchfolk!" Then some ran to escape or to bar their doors, and others scurried to save their market goods, and those fleeing were trapped in the square by those coming to see what was going on, and there was panic and havoc, stalls over-turned, canopies dragging, frightened horses plunging and trampling, cattle bawling, the farmers of Caspro-mant brandishing their lances and cudgels at fishwives and tinsmiths. Canoc called them out of this panic, threatening not the townspeople but his own men with his power, till he got them gathered around him, some of them doggedly hanging on to goods they had grabbed from the market stalls—a pink shawl, a copper stew pot.

He told me, "I saw that in a blood-fight, we were lost. There were hundreds of those folk—hundreds!"

How could he have known what a town was? He had never seen one.

"If we went into the houses to loot, we'd be sepa-rated and they'd pick us off one by one. Only Ternoc and I had a gift strong enough to attack or defend with. And what were we to take? There was all this stuff, things, everywhere—food, goods, clothes, no end to it! How could we take all that? What were we after? I wanted me a wife, but I didn't see how that was to be, the way things were there. And the one thing we really need in the Uplands is hands to work. I knew if I didn't put a scare into them, and soon, they'd be all over us. So I raised up the parley flag, hoping they knew what it was. They did. Some men showed themselves at the windows of the big house over the marketplace and waved a cloth out the window.

"Then I called out, 'I am Canoc Caspro of the True Lineage of Caspromant, and I have the gift and power to undo, which you shall see me use.' And first I struck one of the market stalls, so it fell all to pieces. Then I turned half round, to be sure they saw what I did and how I did it, and I struck the corner of a big stone building across from the house they were in. I held my arm out steady, so they could see. They saw the wall of the building move and bulge, and stones slip down out of it, making a hole in the wall. That grew bigger, and the sacks of grain inside burst open, and the noise of the stones falling was terrible. 'Enough, enough!' they shouted out. So I ceased to unmake the granary and turned to them again. They wanted to talk and parley.

They asked me what I wanted of them. I said, 'Women and boys.'

"There went up an awful howl at that. People in all the streets and houses around shouted, 'No! No! Kill the witches!' There were so many of them, their voices were like a storm of wind. My horse jumped and screamed. An arrow had just nicked his rump. I looked up into the window above the one where the men were parleying and saw an archer leaning far out the window to draw his bow again. I struck him. His body fell like a sack from the window to the stones below, and burst. Then I saw a man at the edge of the crowd of people caught in the marketplace stoop and come up with a stone in his hand, and I struck him. I unmade his arm only. It fell to his side limp as a string. He began to scream, and there was wailing and panic where the archer had fallen. 'I will unmake the next man who moves,' I called aloud. And nobody moved."

Canoc kept his men close around while he parleyed. Ternoc guarded his back. The men speaking for the town consented, under his threats, to give him five serf women and five boys. They began to argue for time to collect the tribute, as they called it, but that he forbade:

"Send them here, now, and we will choose what we want," he said, and raised his left hand a little, at which they agreed to his demand.

Then came a time that seemed very long to him, while the crowds in the side streets ebbed and then grew again, pressing closer, and he could do nothing but sit his sweating horse and keep a keen eye out for archers and other threats. At last dismal little groups of boys and women came driven through the streets to the marketplace, two here and three there, weeping and pleading, some even crawling on their hands and knees, goaded forward by whips and kicks. There were five boys in all, none of them more than ten years old, and four women: two little serf girls half dead with fear, and two older women with stained, stinking clothing who came without being driven, maybe thinking life among the witchfolk could not be worse than life as a tanner's slave. And that was all.

Canoc thought it unwise to insist on a better selection to choose from. The longer he was here so hugely outnumbered, the nearer to the time when somebody in the mob of people shot an arrow or threw a stone that hit its mark, and then the crowd would tear them all to pieces.

All the same, he would not be bilked by these merchants.

"There are four women only," he said.

The parleyers whined and argued.

His time was short. He looked about the market-place and the big houses around it. He saw a woman's face in the window of a narrow house at the corner. She wore a willow-green color that had caught his eye before. She was not hiding, but standing right in the window looking down at him.

"Her," he said, pointing. He pointed with his right hand, but all the people gasped and cowered. That made him laugh. He moved his right hand slowly across the watching faces in a pretense of unmaking them all.

The door of the corner house opened, and the woman in willow-green came out and stood on the step. She was young, small, and thin. Her long hair lay black on her green gown.

"Will you be my wife?" Canoc said to her.

She stood still. "Yes," she said, and came walking slowly across the ruined marketplace to him. She wore strapped black slippers. He held his left hand down to her. She stepped in the stirrup, and he swung her up into the saddle before him.

"The mules and their gear are yours!" he called out to the townsmen, mindful of the gift's gift. From his poverty it was indeed a great gift, though the people of Dunet may well have taken it for a final insolence.

His men had each taken one of the serfs up to ride double with them, and so they set out, riding sedately, in order, the crowds falling away from them in silence, through the street, out from between the house walls, onto the northern road, seeing the mountains before them.

So ended the last raid on the Lowlands from Caspromant. Neither Canoc nor his bride ever went down that road again.

She was named Melle Aulitta. She owned the willow-green dress, the little black slippers she stood in, and a tiny opal on a silver chain around her neck. That was her dowry. He married her four nights after he brought her home to the Stone House. His mother and the housewomen had readied clothing and other things proper for a bride to have, in great haste and with a good will. Brantor Orrec married them in the hall of the Stone House, with all the members of the raiding troop present, and all the people of Caspromant, and whoever could come from the domains of the west to dance at the wedding.

"And then," I said, when my father had finished the story, "Mother had me!"

◆ ◆ ◆

MELLE AULITTA was born and grew up in Derris Water, fourth of the five daughters of a priest-magistrate of the civic religion of Bendraman. It is a high office, and the priest-magistrate and his wife were well off, bringing up their daughters in leisure and luxury, though very strictly, for the state religion demands modesty, chastity, and obedience of women, and is full of penances and humiliations for those who disobey. Adild Aulitta was a kindly and indulgent father. His highest hope for his girls was that they should be dedicated virgins in the City Temple. Melle was taught reading, writing, some mathematics, a great deal of holy history and poetry, and the elements of urban surveying and architecture, as preparation for that honorable career. She liked learning and was an excellent pupil.

But when she was eighteen, something went awry; something occurred, I don't know what; she never said; she only smiled and passed over the matter. Maybe her tutor fell in love with her and she was blamed for it. Maybe she had a sweetheart and stole out to meet him. Maybe it was a smaller matter even than that. Not the least shadow of a scandal may touch a postulant virgin of the City Temple, on whose purity the prosperity of all Bendraman depends. I have wondered if Melle may have engineered a little scandal in order to escape the City Temple. In any case, she was sent to stay with distant cousins in the north, in the remote and rural town of Dunet. They too were respectable, proper people, who kept her closer than ever while they bargained and chicaned with local families for a suitable husband for her and brought the candidates in to look her over.

"One of them," she said, "was a little fat man with a pink nose, who trafficked in pigs. Another of them was a tall, tall, thin, thin boy who prayed for an hour eleven times a day. He wanted me to pray with him."

So she looked out of the window, and saw Canoc of Caspromant astride his red stallion, destroying men and houses with a glance. As he chose her, she chose him.

"How did you make your cousins let you go?" I asked, knowing the answer, savoring it in advance.

"They were all lying down on the floor, under the furniture, so that the witch warrior couldn't see them and melt their bones and destroy them. I said, 'Don't fear, Cousin. Is it not said, *a virgin shall save thy house and goods?*' And I went downstairs and outside."

"How did you know Father wouldn't destroy you?"

"I knew," she said.

• • •

SHE HAD NO MORE idea of where she was going and what she was getting into than Canoc had when he rode down out of the mountains expecting Dunet to be like our villages—a few huts and hovels, a cattle pen, and nine or ten inhabitants, all gone hunting. Probably she thought she was going to something not very different from her father's house, or at least her cousin's house, a cleanly, warm, bright place, full of company and comforts. How could she have known?

To Lowlanders, the Uplands are an accursed, forgotten corner of a world they left behind long ago. They know nothing of them. A warlike people might have sent an army up to clear out these fearsome, irksome remnants of the past, but Bendraman and Urdile are lands of merchants, farmers, scholars, and priests, not warriors. All they did was turn their back on the mountains and forget them. Even in Dunet, my mother said, many people no longer believed in the tales of the Men of the Carrantages—goblin hordes sweeping down on the cities of the plain, monsters on horseback, who set whole fields aflame with a sweep of the hand and withered an army with a glance of the eye. All that was long ago, "when Cumbelo was King." Nothing like that happened these days. People used to trade from Dunet for the fine cream-white Upland cattle, they told her, but the breed had all but died out. The land was terribly poor up there. Nobody lived on the old Upland domains but poor herdsmen and shepherds and farmers scratching a living out of stone.

And that was, as my mother found, the truth. Or a substantial part of it.

But there were many kinds of truth in my mother's view of things, as many kinds as there were tales to tell.

All the adventures in the stories she told us as children happened "when Cumbelo was King." The brave young priest-knights who defeated devils in the shape of huge dogs, the fearsome witchfolk of the Carrantages, the talking fish that warned of earthquake, the beggar girl who got a flying cart made out of moonlight, they were all of the time when Cumbelo was King. The rest of her stories were not adventures at all, except for that one, the story in which she herself stepped out of a door and walked across a marketplace. There the two lines of story crossed, the two truths met.

Her stories without adventures were mere descriptions of the tame doings of a stuffy household in a middle-sized city in a sleepy country of the Lowlands. I loved them as well or better than the adventures. I demanded them: Tell about Derris Water! And I think she liked to talk about it not only to please me but to tease and appease her homesickness. She was always a stranger among strange folk, however much she loved them and was beloved. She was merry, joyous, active, full of life; but I know one of her greatest happinesses was to curl up with me on rugs and cushions in front of the small hearth in her sitting room, the round room in the tower, and tell me what they sold in the markets of Derris Water. She told how she and her sisters used to spy on their father getting dressed in all his corsets and paddings and robes and overrobes as priest-magistrate, and how he wobbled walking in the high-soled shoes that made him taller than other men, and how, when he took off the shoes and robes, he shrank. She told how she had gone with family friends on a boat that sailed clear down the Trond to its mouth where it ran out into the sea. She told me of the sea. She told me that the snailstones we found in quarries and used for gaming pieces were living creatures down on the ocean shore, delicate, colored, shining.

My father would come in from his farm work to her

room—with clean hands, and in clean shoes, for she held firmly to certain principles new to the Stone House—and he would sit with us, listening. He loved to listen to her. She talked like a little stream running, clearly and merrily, with the Lowland softness and fluency. To people in the cities, talk is an art and a pleasure, not a matter of mere use and need. She brought that art and pleasure to Caspromant. She was the light of my father's eyes.

♦ 4 ♦

Feuds and bonds among the Upland lineages went back before memory, before history, before reason. Caspro and Drum had always been at odds. Caspro, Rodd, and Barre had always been friendly, or friendly enough to mend their feuds after a while.

While Drum had prospered, largely by sheep stealing and land grabbing, these last three families had come on hard times. Their great days seemed to be behind them, especially the Caspros. Even in Blind Caddard's time the strength and numbers of our line had grown perilously small, though we still held our domain and some thirty families of serfs and farmers.

A farmer had some ancestral relation to a lineage, though not necessarily the gift; a serf had neither. Both had the obligation of fealty and the right of claim on the chief family of their domain. The family of most serfs and farmers had lived on the land they farmed as long as the brantor's family or longer. The work and management of crops, livestock, forests, and all the rest were allocated by long custom and frequent council. The people of our domain were seldom reminded that the brantor had power of life or death over them. Caddard's gift of two serfs to Tibro had been a rare and reckless assertion of wealth and power, which saved the domain by catching the invaders in the net of his extravagant generosity. The gift's gift was stronger, perhaps, than the gift itself. Caddard had used it wisely. But things had gone far wrong when a brantor used his power against his own people, as Erroy did at Geremant, and Ogge at Drummant.

The Barre gift had never been very useful for such purposes. To be able to call wild beasts out of the forest, or gentle a colt, or discuss things with a hound, was a gift indeed; but it did not give you dominion over men who could set your haystack afire or kill you and your hound with a glance and a word. The Barres had lost their own domain long ago to the Helvars of the Carrantages. Various families of the lineage had come down the mountain and married into our western domains. They tried to keep their line true so as not to weaken or lose their gift, but of course they could not always do so. Several of our farmers were Barres. Our healers and curers of livestock, our hen keepers and hound trainers, were all farmwives with Barre blood in them. There were still Barres of the true line at Geremant, Cordemant, and Roddmant.

The Rodds, with their gift of the knife, were well prepared to defend or to attack and to assert dominion if they wished, but they mostly lacked the temper for it. They were not feuders. They were more interested in elk hunts than in forays. Unlike most self-respecting Uplanders, they would rather breed good cattle than steal them. The cream-white oxen Caspromant had once been famous for had in fact been bred by the Rodds. My ancestors stole cows and bull calves from Roddmant till they had a breeding herd of their own. The Rodds worked their land and bred their cattle and throve well enough, but did not increase and grow great. They had intermarried a good deal with Barres, and so it was that when I was a child, Roddmant had two brantors, Gry's mother Parn Barre and her father Ternoc Rodd.

Our families had been on good terms, as these things go in the Uplands, for generations, and Ternoc and my father were true friends. Ternoc had ridden his droop-lipped farmhorse in the great raid on Dunet. His share of the loot was one of the little serf girls, whom he soon gave to Bata Caspro of Cordemant, who had the other one, because the two were sisters and kept sniveling after each other. The year before the raid, Ternoc and Parn had married. Parn had grown up at Roddmant and had some Rodd blood in her. A month after my mother gave birth to me, Parn bore a daughter, Gry.

Gry and I were cradle friends. When we were little children our parents visited often, and we ran off and played. I was the first, I think, to see Gry's gift come to power, though I am not certain if it is a memory or the imagination of something she told me. Children can see what they are told. What I see is this: Gry and I are sitting making twig houses in the dirt at the side of Roddmant kitchen gardens, and a bull elk, a great stag, comes out of the little wood that lies behind the house. He walks to us. He is immense, taller than a house, with great, swaying branches of antlers that balance against the sky. He comes slowly and directly to Gry. She reaches up and he puts his nose to her palm as if in salute. "Why did he come here?" I ask, and she says, "I called him." That is all I remember.

When I told my father the memory, years later, he said it could not have been so. Gry and I had been no more than four, and a gift, he said, scarcely ever shows itself till the child is nine or ten years old.

"Caddard was three," I said.

My mother touched the side of my little finger with the side of her little finger: *Do not contradict your father.* Canoc was tense and anxious, I was careless and bumptious; she protected him from me and me from him, with the most delicate, imperceptible tact.

Gry was the best of playmates. We got into a lot of mild trouble. The worst was when we let the chickens out. Gry claimed she could teach chickens to do all sorts of tricks—walk across lines, jump up onto her finger. "It is my gift," she said pompously. We were six or seven. We went into the big poultry yard at Roddmant and cornered some half-grown poults and tried to teach them something—anything—anything at all: an occupation so frustrating and absorbing that we never noticed we had left the yard gate wide open until all the hens had followed the rooster right up into the woods. Then everyone had a try at rounding them all back up. Parn, who could have called them, was away on a hunt. The foxes were grateful to us, if no one else was. Gry felt very guilty, the poultry yard being one of her charges. She wept as I never saw her weep again. She roamed in the woods all that evening and the next day, calling the missing hens, "Biddy! Lily! Snowy! Fan!" in a little voice like a disconsolate quail.

We always seemed to get into mischief at Rodd-mant. When Gry came with her parents or her father to Caspromant, there were no disasters. My mother was very fond of Gry. She would say suddenly, "Stand there, Gry!" Gry would stand still, and my mother would gaze at her till the seven-year-old became self-conscious and began to wriggle and giggle. "Now be still," my mother would say. "I'm learning you, don't you see, so that I can have a girl of my own exactly like you. I want to know how to do it."

"You could have another boy like Orrec," Gry offered, but my mother said, "No! One Orrec is quite enough. I need a Gry!"

Gry's mother Parn was a strange, restless woman. Her gift was strong, and she seemed half a wild creature herself. She was much in demand to call animals to hunters, and was often away, half across the Uplands, at a hunt at one domain or another. When she was at Roddmant she seemed always to have a cage around her, to be looking at you through bars. She and her husband Ternoc were polite and wary with each other. She had no particular interest in her daughter, whom she treated like all other children, with impartial indifference.

"Does your mother teach you how to use your gift?" I asked Gry once, in the self-importance of being taught by my father how to use my gift.

Gry shook her head. "She says you don't use the gift. It uses you."

"You have to learn how to control it," I informed her, solemn and severe.

"I don't," said Gry.

She was wilful, indifferent—too much like her mother, sometimes. She would not argue with me, would not defend her opinion, would not change it. I wanted words. She wanted silence. But when my mother told stories, Gry listened from her silence, and heard every word, heard, held, treasured, pondered it.

"You're a listener," Melle said to her. "Not just a caller, a listener too. You listen to mice, don't you?"

Gry nodded.

"What do they say?"

"Mouse things," Gry said. She was very shy, even with Melle, whom she loved dearly.

"I suppose, being a caller, you could call the mice that are nesting in my storeroom and suggest to them that they go live in the stable?"

Gry thought about it.

"They would have to move the babies," she said.

"Ah," said my mother. "I never thought. Out of the question. Besides, there's the stable cat."

"You could bring the cat to your storeroom," Gry said. Her mind moved unpredictably; she saw as the mice saw, as the cat saw, as my mother saw, all at once. Her world was unfathomably complex. She did not defend her opinions, because she held conflicting opinions on almost everything. And yet she was immovable.

"Could you tell about the girl who was kind to the ants?" she asked my mother, timidly, as if it were a great imposition.

"The girl who was kind to the ants," my mother repeated, as if reciting a title. She closed her eyes.

She had told us that many of her stories came from a book she had had as a child, and that when she told them, she felt as if she were reading from the book. The first time she told us that, Gry asked, "What is a book?"

So my mother read to us from the book that was not there.

Long, long ago, when Cumbelo was King, a widow lived in a village with her four daughters. And they went along well enough till the woman fell ill and couldn't get over it. So a wise woman came and looked her over and said, "Nothing can cure you but a drink of the water of the Well of the Sea."

"Oh me, oh me, then I'll surely die," says the widow, "for how can I go to that well, sick as I am?"

"Haven't you four daughters?" says the wise woman.

So the widow begged her eldest daughter to go to the Well of the Sea and fetch a cup of that water. "And you shall have all my love," she said, "and my best bonnet."

So the eldest girl went out, and she walked a while, and sat down to rest, and where she sat she saw a huddle of ants trying to drag a dead wasp to their nest. "Ugh, the nasty things," she said, and crushed them under her heel, and went on. It was a long way to the shore of the sea, but she trudged along and got there, and there was the sea with its great waves bashing and crashing on the sand. "Oh, that's enough of that!" said the girl, and she dipped her cup into the nearest wave and carried the water home. "Here's the water, Mother," says she, and the mother takes and drinks it. Oh, bitter it was, salt and bitter! Tears came to the mother's eyes. But she thanked the girl and gave her her best bonnet. And the girl went out in the bonnet, and soon enough she caught her a sweetheart.

But the mother grew sicker than ever, so she asked her second daughter to go fetch her water from the Well of the Sea, and if she did she could have her mother's love and her best lace gown. So the girl went. On the way she sat down to rest, and saw a man plowing with an ox, and saw the yoke was riding wrong, galling a great sore on the ox's neck. But that was nothing to her. She went on and came to the shore of the sea. There it was with its great waves roaring and boring on the sand. "Oh, that's enough of that!" says she, and dips the cup in quick, and home she trots. "Here's the water, Mother, now give me the gown." Salt, salt and bitter that water was, so the mother could scarcely swallow it. As soon as she went out in the lace gown the girl found her a sweetheart, but the mother lay as if under the hand of death. She hardly had breath to ask the third girl to go. "The water I drank can't be the water of the Well of the Sea," she said, "for it was bitter brine. Go, and you shall have all my love."

"I don't care for that, but give me the house over your head and I'll go," says the third daughter.

And the mother said she would. So the girl set off with a good will, straight to the seashore, never stopping. Just on the sand dunes she met a grey goose with a broken wing. It came to meet her, dragging its wing. "Get away, stupid thing," the girl said, and down to the sea she goes, and sees the great waves thundering and blundering on the sand. "Oh, that's enough of that!" says the girl, and pops her cup in, and back home she goes. And as soon as her mother tasted the bitter cup of salt sea brine, "Now, out you go, Mother," says the girl, "this is my house now."

"Will you not let me die in my own bed, child?"

"If you'll be quick about it," says the girl. "But hurry up, for the lad next door wants to marry me for my property, and my sisters and I are going to have a grand wedding here in my house."

So the mother lay dying, weeping salt and bitter tears. The youngest of her daughters came to her softly and said, "Don't cry, Mother. I'll go get you a drink of that water."

"It's no use, child. It's too far, you're too young, I have nothing left to give you, and I must die."

"Well, I'll try all the same," says the girl, and off she goes.

As she walked along she saw some ants by the roadside, trying to carry the bodies of their comrades, struggling along. "Here, that's easier for me to do," says the girl, and she scooped them all up in her hand and carried them to their ant hill and set them down there.

She walked along and saw an ox plowing with a yoke that galled it till it bled. "I'll set that yoke straight," she said to the plowman, and she made a pad of her apron to go under the yoke, and set it to ride easier on the ox's neck.

She walked a long way and came at last to the shore, and there on the dunes of sand stood a grey goose with a broken wing. "Ah, poor bird," says the girl, and she took off her overskirt and tore it up and bound the goose's wing so it might heal.

Then she went down to the edge of the sea. There the great waves lay shining. She tasted the seawater and it was salt and bitter. Far out over the waters was an island, a mountain on the shining water. "How can I come to the Well of the Sea?" she said. "I can never swim so far." But she took off her shoes and was walking into the sea to swim, when she heard a cloppity, clop, and over the sand came a great white ox with silver horns. "Come," says the ox, "climb up, I'll carry you." So she climbed on the ox's back and held its horns, and into the water they went, and the ox swam till they came to the far island.

The rocks of the island were steep as walls and smooth as glass. "How shall I come to the Well of the Sea?" she said. "I can never climb so high." But she reached up to try to climb the rocks. A grey goose greater than an eagle came flying down to her. "Come," says the grey goose, "climb up, I'll carry you." So she got up between its wings, and it bore her up to the peak of the island. And there was a deep well of clear water. She dipped her cup in it. And the grey goose bore her back across the sea, while the white ox swam after.

But when the grey goose set foot upon the sand, he stood up a man, a tall, fine young man. And the strips of her skirt hung from his right arm.

"I am the baron of the sea," he said, "and I would marry you."

"First I must carry the water to my mother," the girl said.

So he and she both mounted the white ox, and they rode back to the village. Her mother lay there in death's hand. But she swallowed one drop of the water, and raised her head. Another drop, and she sat up. Another drop, and she stood up. Another drop, and she danced.

"It is the sweetest water of all the world," she said. Then she and her youngest daughter and the baron of the sea rode away on the white ox to his palace of silver, where he and the girl were married, and the widow danced at the wedding.

"But the ants," Gry whispered.

"Oh, the ants," said my mother. "So, were the ants ungrateful? No! For they came to the wedding too, all crawling along as fast as they could go, and they brought with them a golden ring, which had lain a hundred years under the ground in their ant hill, and with that ring the young man and the youngest daughter were married!"

"Last time," said Gry.

"Last time?"

"Last time, you said…you said the ants went and ate all the cakes and sweet things at the older sisters' wedding."

"They did. They did that, too. Ants can do a great many things, and they're everywhere at once," my mother said earnestly, and then broke into laughter, and we all laughed, because she had forgotten the ants.

Gry's question, "What is a book?" had made my mother think about some matters that had been neglected or ignored in the Stone House. Nobody at Caspromant could read or write, and we counted sheep with a notched stick. It was no shame to us, but it was to her. I don't know if she ever dreamed of going back home for a visit, or of people of her family coming to the Uplands; it was most unlikely that either should happen; but what about the children? What if her son were to go down into the rest of the world, untaught, as ignorant as a beggar of the city streets? Her pride would not endure it.

There were no books in the Uplands, so she made them. She glazed fine linen squares and stretched them between rollers. She made ink of oak galls, pens of goose quills. She wrote out a primer for us and taught us to read it. She taught us to write, first with sticks in the dust, then with quills on stretched linen, holding our breath, scratching and spattering horribly. She washed the pale ink out, and we could write again. Gry found it all very hard, and kept to it only through her love for my mother. I found it the easiest thing in the world.

"Write me a book!" I demanded, and so Melle wrote down the life of Raniu for me. She took her charge seriously. Given her education, she felt that if I had only one book, it should be a holy history. She remembered some of the phrases and language of the *History of the Acts and Miracles of Lord Raniu*, and told the rest in her own words. She gave me the book on my ninth birthday: forty squares of glazed linen, covered edge to edge in pale, formal script, sewn with blue-dyed thread along the top. I pored over it. When I knew it all by heart, still I read and reread it, treasuring the written words not only for the story they told but for what I saw hidden in them: all the other stories. The stories my mother told. And the stories no one had ever told.

✦ 5 ✦

During these years, my father also continued my education; but as I showed no signs of being a second Caddard and terrifying the world with my untimely powers, he could only tell me and show me the ways of our gift, and wait in patience till it showed itself in me. He himself had been nine years old, he said, before he could knock a gnat down. He was not a patient man by nature, only by self-discipline, and he was hopeful. He tested me pretty often. I tried my best, glaring and pointing and whispering, summoning up that mysterious thing, my will.

"What is the will?" I asked him.

"Well, it's your intention. You must mean to use your gift. If you used it without willing to, you might do great harm."

"But what does it feel like, to use it?"

He frowned and thought a long time before he spoke.

"It's as if something comes all together," he said. His left hand moved a little, involuntarily. "As if you were a knot at the center of a dozen lines, all of them drawn into you, and you holding them taut. As if you were a bow, but with a dozen bowstrings. And you draw them in tighter, and they draw on you, till you say, 'Now!' And the power shoots out like the arrow."

"So you will your power to go unmake the thing you're looking at?"

He frowned again and thought again. "It's not a matter you can say in words. There's no words in it at all."

"But you say…How do you know what to say?"

For I had realised that what Canoc said when he used his gift was never the same word, and maybe not a word at all. It sounded like the *hah!* or hard outbreath of a man making a great, sudden effort with his whole body, yet there was more in it than that; but I could never imitate it.

"It comes when…It's part of the power acting," was all he could say. A conversation like this troubled him. He could not answer such questions. I should not ask them; I should not have to ask them.

As I turned twelve, and thirteen, I worried increasingly that my gift had not shown itself. My fear was not only in my thoughts but in my dreams, in which I was always just about to do a great, dreadful act of destruction, to bring a huge stone tower crumbling and crashing down, to unmake all the people of some dark, strange village—or I had just done it, and was struggling among ruins and faceless, boneless corpses to find my way home. But always it was before the act of undoing, or after it.

I would wake from such a nightmare, my heart pounding like a horse at the gallop, and try to master my terror and gather the power together, as Canoc had said to do. Shivering so that I could scarcely breathe, I would stare at the carved knob at the foot of my bed, just visible in the dawn light, and raise up my left hand and point at it, and determine to destroy that black knob of wood, and push out my breath in a convulsive *hah!* Then I would shut my eyes hard and pray the darkness that my wish, my will had been granted. But when I opened my eyes at last, the wooden knob stood untouched. My time had not come.

Before my fourteenth year we had had little to do with the people of Drummant. The neighbor with whom we were on terms of watchful enmity was Erroy of Geremant. Gry and I were utterly forbidden to go anywhere near our border with that domain, which ran through an ash wood. We obeyed. We both knew Bent Gonnen, and the man with his arms on backwards. Brantor Erroy had done that in one of his fits of joking—he called it joking. The man was one of his own serfs. "Took the use right out of him," our farmers said, "a strange way to do." That was about as far as criticism of a brantor went. Erroy was mad, but nobody said so. They kept quiet and steered clear.

And Erroy kept away from Caspromant. True, he had twisted our serf Gonnen's back, but Gonnen, whatever he said, had almost certainly been over the line, stealing wood from Geremant. It was, by the code of the Uplands, justification of a sort. My father took no revenge, but went up to the ash wood and waited till Erroy came by and could see what he did. Then Canoc summoned up his power and drew a line of destruction straight across the wood, following the border line, as if

a lightning bolt had run parallel to the ground destroying everything in its path, leaving a fence of dead, ashen,
black-leaved trees. He said nothing to Erroy, who was
lurking in the upper edge of the wood, watching. Erroy
said nothing, but he was never seen near the boundary
wood again.

Since the raid on Dunet, my father's reputation as a
dangerous man was secure. It did not need this spectac-
ular act of warning to confirm it. "Quick with the eye is
Caspro," people said. I was savagely proud when I heard
them say it. Proud of him, of us, of our line, our power.

Geremant was a poor, misrun domain, not much
to worry about; but Drummant was something else.
Drummant was wealthy and growing wealthier. The
Drums fancied themselves to be brantors of the
Carrantages, people said, with all their airs and arrogance, demanding protection payment here and tribute
there—tribute, as if they were overlords of the Uplands! Yet weaker domains ended up buying them off,
paying the tribute of sheep or cattle or wool or even
serfs that Drum extorted; for the gift of that line was a
fearful one. It was slow to act, invisible in action, it
lacked the drama of the knife, the undoing, the fire; but
Ogge of Drummant could walk across your field and

pasture, and next year the corn would wither in the ground, and no grass would grow again for years. He could lay the blight on a flock of sheep, a herd of cattle, a household.

They had all died at Rimmant, a little domain that lay along the southwest border of Drummant. Brantor Ogge had gone there with his demands. The Brantor of Rimm had met him at the door, defiant, ready to use his power of fire throwing, and told him to begone. But Ogge crept round their house at night and made his spells, so they said—for his power was not a matter of a glance and a word, but of whispering and naming and passes of the hands, that took some time to weave. And from that time, every soul of the family of Rimm had sickened, and in four years all were dead.

Canoc doubted this story as it was commonly told. "Drum couldn't do that, in darkness, he outdoors and they in," he said with certainty. "His power is like ours, it works through the seeing eye. Maybe he left some poison there. Maybe they died of illness that was nothing to do with him." But however it happened, Ogge was seen as the cause of it, and certainly got the profit of it, adding Rimmant to his properties.

All this did not concern us directly for a long time.

Then the two Corde brothers fell to feuding over who was heir and true brantor of their domain, and Ogge moved some of his people into the southern half of Cordemant, claiming that he was protecting it. The brothers went on quarreling and making claims, fools that they were, while Ogge took over the best part of their land. And that brought Drummant right up against Caspromant, along our southwest border. Now Ogge was our neighbor.

From that time on my father's temper took a turn towards darkness. He felt that we, all the people of his domain, were at risk, and that we had only him to defend us. His sense of responsibility was strong, perhaps exaggerated. To him, privilege was obligation; command was service; power, the gift itself, entailed a heavy loss of freedom. If he had been a young man without wife or child, I think he might have mounted a foray against Drummant, running all the risks at once, staking himself on one free act; but he was a householder, a burdened man, full of the cares of managing a poor estate and looking after its people, with a defenseless wife and no kinsman of his gift to stand with him, except, perhaps, his son.

There was the screw that tightened his anxiety. His

son was thirteen years old now and still had shown no sign of his gift.

I had been trained perfectly in the use of it, but I had nothing to use. It was as if I had been taught to ride without ever getting up on a horse's back.

That this worried Canoc sharply and increasingly I knew, for he could not hide it. In this matter, Melle could not be the help and solace to him that she was in everything else, nor could she mediate between the two of us or lessen the load we laid on each other. For what did she know of the gift and the ways it took? It was entirely foreign to her. She was not of Upland blood. She had never seen Canoc use his power but that once, in the marketplace of Dunet, when he killed one attacker and maimed another. He had no wish to show her his power to destroy, and no call to. It frightened her; she did not understand it, perhaps only half believed it.

After he left the line of dead trees in the ash wood to warn Erroy, he had used his power only in small ways to show me how it was done and the cost of doing it. He never used it to hunt game, for the disruption and collapse of the animal's flesh and bones and organs left a horror no one would think of eating. In any event, to his mind, the gift was not for commonplace usage but for real need only. So Melle could more or less forget he had it, and saw no great reason to worry if I didn't have it.

Indeed, it was only when—at last—she heard that I had shown my power that she was alarmed.

And so was I.

◆ ◆ ◆

I WAS OUT RIDING with my father, he on the old grey stallion and I on Roanie. With us came Alloc, a young farmer. Alloc was of Caspro lineage through his father, and had "a touch of the eye"—he could unknot knots and a few such tricks. Maybe he could kill a rat if he stared long enough, he said, but he'd never found a rat willing to stay around long enough for him to make sure. He was a good-natured man with a love of horses and a hand with them, the trainer my father had long hoped for. He was on Roanie's last colt. We were train-ing that two-year-old carefully, for my father saw reborn in him the tall red horse he rode to Dunet.

We were out on the southwestern sheep grazings of our domain, keeping an eye out, though Canoc didn't say so, for any sign of men from Drummant straying on our land, or their sheep mixed in among our flocks so that Drum's shepherds could "reclaim" some of ours when they rounded up theirs—a trick we had been warned of by the Cordes, who had long had Drum for a neighbor. We did indeed spot some strangers in among our wiry, rough-wooled Upland ewes. Our shepherds put a spot of yellow-onion stain on the woolly ear so we could tell our sheep from Erroy's, who used to let Gere sheep stray onto our grazing and then claim we had stolen them—though he had not done so since my father marked the ash grove.

We turned south to find our shepherd and his dogs and tell him to cut the Drum sheep out and send them back where they belonged. Then we rode west again to find the break in the fence and get it mended. A black frown was on Canoc's face. Alloc and I came along meek and silent behind him. We were going a pretty good gait along the hillside when Greylag put a forefoot onto slick slate rock hidden by grass and slipped, making a great lurch. The horse recovered, and Canoc kept his seat. He was swinging off to see if Greylag had strained his leg, when I saw on the slanting stone where his foot would touch down an adder poised to strike. I shouted and pointed, Canoc paused half off the horse, looked at me, at the snake, swung his left hand free and towards it, and recovered his seat on the horse, all in a moment. Greylag made a big, four-footed hop away from the adder.

It lay on the stone like a cast-off sock, limp and misshapen.

Alloc and I both sat on our horses staring, frozen, our left hands out stiffly pointing at the snake.

Canoc quieted Greylag and dismounted carefully. He looked at the ruined thing on the rock. He looked up at me. His face was strange: rigid, fierce.

"Well done, my son," he said.

I sat in my saddle, stupid, staring.

"Well done indeed!" said Alloc, with a big grin. "By the Stone, but that's a wicked great poisonous pissant of a snake and it might have bit the Brantor to the bone!"

I stared at my father's muscular, brown, bare legs.

Alloc dismounted to look at the remains of the adder, for the red colt wouldn't go near it. "Now that's destroyed," he said. "A strong eye did that! Look there, that's its poison fangs. Foul beast," and he spat. "A strong eye," he said again.

I said, "I didn't—"

I looked at my father, bewildered.

"The snake was unmade when I saw it," Canoc said.

"But you—"

He frowned, though not in anger. "It was you that struck it," he said.

"It was," Alloc put in. "I saw you do it, Young Orrec. Quick as lightning."

"But I—"

Canoc watched me, stern and intent.

I tried to explain. "But it was like all the other times, when I tried—when nothing happened." I stopped. I wanted to cry, with the suddenness of the event, and my confusion, for it seemed I had done something I did not know I had done. "It didn't feel any different," I said in a choked voice.

My father continued to gaze at me for a moment; then he said, "It was, though." And he swung up onto Greylag again. Alloc had to catch the red colt, which didn't want to be remounted. The strange moment passed. I did not want to look at what had been the snake.

We rode on to the line fence and found where the Drum sheep had crossed; it looked as if stones had been pulled out of the wall recently. We spent the morning rebuilding the wall there and in nearby places where it could use a bit of mending.

I was still so incredulous of what I had done that I could not think about it, and was taken by surprise when, that evening, my father spoke of it to my mother. He was brief and dry, as was his way, and it took her a little while to understand that he was telling her that I had shown my gift and maybe saved his life by doing so. Then she, like me, was too bewildered to respond with pleasure or praise, or anything but anxiety. "Are they so dangerous then, these adders?" she said more than once. "I didn't know they were so venomous. They might be anywhere on the hills where the children run about!"

"They are," Canoc said. "They always have been. Not many of them, fortunately."

That our life was imminently and continually in danger was something Canoc knew as a fact, and something Melle had to struggle reluctantly, against her heart, to believe. She was no fool of hope, but she had always been sheltered from physical harm. And Canoc sheltered her, though he never lied to her.

"They gave the old name to our gift," he said now. "'The adder,' people used to call it." He glanced at me, just the flick of an eye, grave and hard as he had been ever since the instant on the hillside. "Their venom and our stroke act much the same way."

She winced. After a while she said to him, "I know you're glad the gift has run true." It took courage for her to say it.

"I never doubted that it did," he replied. That was said as reassurance to her and to me also, but I am not sure either of us was able to accept it.

I lay awake that night as long as a boy that age can lie awake, going over and over what had happened when I saw the adder, becoming more and more con-fused and troubled. I slept at last, to dream confused and troubled dreams, and woke very early. I got up and went down to the stables. For once I was there before my father; but he soon came, yawning, rubbing sleep out of his eyes. "Hello, Orrec," he said.

"Father," I said, "I want to— About the snake."

He cocked his head a bit.

"I know I used my hand and eye. But I don't think I killed it. My will— It wasn't any different. It was just like all the other times." I began to feel an aching pres-sure in my throat and behind my eyes.

"You don't think Alloc did it?" he said. "It's not in him."

"But you— You struck it—"

"It was unmade when I saw it," he said as he had said the day before, but some flicker of consciousness or question or doubt passed through his voice and eyes as he spoke. He considered. The hardness had come back into his face, which had been soft with sleep when I first saw him at the stable doors.

"I struck the snake, yes," he said. "But after you did. I am sure you struck first. And with a quick, strong hand and eye."

"But how will I know when I use my power, if it— if it seems just the same as all the times I tried to and didn't?"

That brought him up short. He stood there, frowning, pondering. Finally he said, almost hesitantly, "Would you try it out, the gift, Orrec, now—on a small thing— on that bit of a weed there?" He pointed to a little clump of dandelions between the stones of the courtyard near the stable door.

I stared at the dandelions. The tears swelled up in me and I could not hold them back. I put my hands over my face and wept. "I don't want to, I don't want to!" I cried. "I can't, I can't, I don't want to!"

He came and knelt and put an arm round me. He let me cry.

"It's all right, my dear," he said when I grew quieter.
"It's all right. It is a heavy thing." And he sent me in to
wash my face.

We spoke no more about the gift then, or for some
while.

✦ 6 ✦

We went back with Alloc for several days after that to mend and build up the fence along our southwest sheep pastures, making it clear to the shepherds on the other side that we knew every stone of those walls and would be aware if one were moved. Along on the third or fourth day of the work, a group of horsemen came towards us up the long falling pastures below the Little Sheer, land that had been the Corde domain and now was Drummant. Sheep trotted away from the riders, blatting hoarsely. The men rode straight at us, their pace increasing as the hilltop leveled. It was a low, misty day. We were sodden with the fine rain that drifted over the hills, and dirty from handling the wet and muddy stones.

"Oh, by the Stone, that's the old adder himself," Alloc muttered. My father shot him a glance that silenced him, and spoke out in a quiet, clear voice as the horsemen cantered right up to the wall—"A good day to you, Brantor Ogge."

All three of us eyed their horses with admiration, for they were fine creatures. The brantor rode a beautiful honey-colored mare who looked too delicate for his bulk. Ogge Drum was a man of about sixty, barrel-girthed and bull-necked. He wore the black kilt and coat, but of fine woven wool, not felt, and his horse's bridle was silver-mounted. His bare calves bulged with muscle. I saw them, mostly, and little of his face, because I did not want to look up into his eyes. All my life I had heard ill of Brantor Ogge; and the way he had ridden straight at us as if in assault, reining in hard just short of the wall, was not reassuring.

"Mending your sheep fence, Caspro?" he said in a big, unexpectedly warm and jovial voice. "A good job too. I have some men good at laying drystone. I'll send them up to help you."

"We're just finishing up today, but I thank you," Canoc said.

"I'll send them up anyhow. Fences have two sides, eh?"

"That they do," my father said. He spoke pleasantly, though his face was as hard as the stone in his hand.

"One of these lads is yours, eh?" Ogge said, surveying Alloc and me. The insult was subtle. He certainly knew that Canoc's son was a boy, not a man of twenty. The implication was that there was no way to tell a Caspro son from a Caspro serf, or so we three took it.

"He is," my father said, and did not name or introduce or even look at me.

"Now that our lands border," said Ogge, "I've had it in mind to come invite you and your lady to visit us at Drummant. If I rode by your house in a day or two, you'd be there?"

"I will," Canoc said. "You are welcome to come."

"Good, good. I'll be by." Ogge raised his hand in a careless, genial salute, wheeled his mare standing, and led his little troop off at a canter along the wall.

"Ah," said Alloc with a sigh, "that's a sweet little yellow mare." He was as thorough a horseman as my father; the two of them longed and schemed to improve our stable. "If we could put Branty to her in a year or two, what a colt that might be!"

"And what a price it would carry," Canoc said harshly.

He was tense and often sullen from that day on. He told my mother to make ready for Ogge's visit, and of course she did so. Then they waited. Canoc did not go far from the Stone House, not wanting her to have to receive Ogge alone. It was half a month before he came.

He brought the same retinue with him, men of his and other lineages of his domain; no women. My father in his stiff pride took that, too, as an insult. He did not let it pass. "I am sorry your wife did not ride with you," he said. Ogge then made apologies and excuses, saying his wife was much burdened with household cares and had been in ill health. "But she looks forward to welcoming you to Drummant," he said, turning to Melle. "In the old days there was far more riding about and visiting from domain to domain. We've let our old Upland customs of cordiality lapse. It's a different matter down in the cities, no doubt, where you have neighbors all about you thick as crows on carrion, as they say."

"Very different," my mother said meekly, eclipsed by his loud voice and big looming body, which seemed always to contain a repressed threat.

"And this would be your lad I saw the other day," he said, suddenly turning on me. "Caddard, is it?"

"Orrec," my mother said, since I was voiceless, though I managed a duck of the head.

"Well, look up, Orrec, let me see your face," the big voice said. "Afraid of the Drum eye, are you?" He laughed again.

My heart was beating at the top of my chest hard enough to choke me, but I made myself hold my head up and look into the big face that hung over me. Ogge's eyes were barely visible under heavy, drooping lids. From those creases and pouches they stared out steady and empty as a snake's eyes.

"And you've shown your gift, I hear." He glanced at my father.

Alloc of course had told everybody on our domain about the adder, and it is amazing how fast word travels from place to place in the Uplands, where it seems that nobody speaks to anybody but their closest kin and not often to them.

"He has," Canoc said, looking at me not at Ogge.

"So it ran true, in spite of everything," Ogge said, in such a warm, congratulatory tone that I could not believe he intended the blatant insult to my mother. "The undoing, now—that's a power I'd like to see! We have only women of the Caspro line at Drummant, as you know. They carry the gift, of course, but can't show it.

Maybe young Orrec here will give us a demonstration. Would you like that, lad?" The big voice was genial, pressing. Refusal was not possible. I said nothing, but in courtesy had to make some response. I nodded.

"Good, then we'll round up some serpents for you before you come, eh? Or you can clear some of the rats and kittens out of our old barn if you like. I'm glad to know the gift runs true"—this to my father with the same booming geniality—"for I've had a thought concerning a granddaughter of mine, my youngest son's daughter, which we might talk about when you come to Drummant." He rose. "Now you've seen I'm not so much an ogre as maybe you've been told"—this to my mother—"you'll do us the honor of a visit, will you, in May, when the roads are dry?"

"With pleasure, sir," Melle said, rising also, and she bowed her head above her hands crossed at the fingertips, a Lowland gesture of polite respect, entirely foreign to us.

Ogge stared at her. It was as if the gesture had made her visible to him. Before that he had not really looked at any of us. She stood there respectful and aloof. Her beauty was unlike that of any Upland woman, a fineness of bone, a quickness, a subtle vigor. I saw his big face change, growing heavy with emotions I could not read—amazement, envy, hunger, hate?

He called to his companions, who had been gathered around the table my mother had set for them. They went out to their horses in the courtyard, and all went jangling off. My mother looked at the ruins of the feast. "They ate well," she said, with a hostess's pride, but also ruefully, for there was nothing left at all for us of the delicacies she had, with much care and work, provided.

"Like crows on carrion," Canoc quoted very drily.

She gave a little laugh. "He's not a diplomat," she said.

"I don't know what he is. Or why he came."

"It seems he came about Orrec."

My father glanced at me, but I stood planted there, determined to hear.

"Maybe," he said, clearly trying to defer the discussion at least until I should not be there to hear it.

My mother had no such scruples. "Was he talking of a betrothal?"

"The girl would be of the right age."

"Orrec's not fourteen!"

"She'd be a little younger. Twelve or thirteen. But a Caspro through her mother, you see."

"Two children betrothed to marry?"

"It is nothing uncommon," Canoc said, his tone getting stiff. "It would be troth only. There'd be no marriage for years."

"It's far too young for any kind of arrangement."

"It can be best to have these things secure and known. A great deal rides on a marriage."

"I won't hear of it," she said quietly, shaking her head. Her tone was not defiant at all, but she did not often declare opposition, and it may have driven my father, tense as he was, farther than he would otherwise have gone.

"I don't know what Drum wants, but if he proposes a betrothal, it's a generous offer, and one we must consider. There is no other girl of the true Caspro lineage in the west." Canoc looked at me, and I could not help but think of how he looked at colts and fillies, with that thoughtful, appraising gaze, seeing what might come of it. Then he turned away and said, "I only wonder why he should propose it. Maybe he means it as a compensation."

Melle stared.

I had to think it out. Did he mean compensation for the three women he might have married to keep his lineage true, the women Ogge had snatched away, driv-

ing him, in defiance, to go and get himself a bride who
was of no lineage at all?

My mother went red, redder than I had ever seen
her, so that the clear brown of her skin was dark as a
winter sunset. She said carefully, "Have you been expecting—compensation?"

Canoc could be as dense as stone. "It would be just,"
he said. "It could mend some fences." He paced down
the room. "Daredan wasn't an old woman. Not too old
to bear Sebb Drum this daughter." He paced back to us
and stood looking down, pondering. "We must consider the offer, if he makes it. Drum is an evil enemy.
He might be a good friend. If it's friendship he offers, I
must take it. And the chance for Orrec is better than I
could hope."

Melle said nothing. She had stated her opposition,
and there was nothing else to say. If the practice of betrothing children was new and distasteful to her, the
principle of making a good marriage for one's child,
the use of marriage for financial and social advantage,
was perfectly familiar to her. And in these matters
of the amity and enmity between domains and the
maintenance of a lineage, she was the foreigner, the
outsider, who must trust my father's knowledge and
judgment.

But I had some ideas of my own, and with my mother there, on my side, I spoke out. "But if I got betrothed to that girl at Drummant," I said, "what about Gry?"

Canoc and Melle both turned and looked at me.

"What about Gry?" Canoc said, with an uncharacteristic pretense of stupidity.

"If Gry and I wanted to get betrothed."

"You're far too young!" my mother burst out, and then saw where that took her.

My father stood silent for some while. "Ternoc and I have talked of this," he said, speaking doggedly, heavily, sentence by sentence. "Gry is of a great line, and strong in her gift. Her mother wishes her to be betrothed to Annren Barre of Cordemant, to keep the lineage true. Nothing has been decided. But this girl at Drummant is of our line, Orrec. That's a matter of very great weight to me, to you, to our people. It's a chance we cannot throw away. Drum is our neighbor now, and kinship is a way to friendship."

"We and Roddmant have *always* been friends," I said, standing my ground.

"I don't discount that." He stood gazing at the despoiled table, undecided for all his decisive speech. "Let

GIFTS

it be for now," he said at last. "Drum may have meant
nothing at all. He blows hot and cold at once. We'll go
there in May and know better what's at stake. It may be
I misunderstood him."

"He is a coarse man, but he seemed to mean to be
friendly," Melle said. "Coarse" was as harsh a word as
she used of anyone. It meant she disliked him very
much. But she was uncomfortable with distrust, which
did not come naturally to her. By seeing goodwill where
there was none, often enough she had created it. The
people of the household worked with and for her with
willing hearts; the sullenest farmers spoke to her cor-
dially, and tight-mouthed old serf women would con-
fide their sorrows to her as to a sister.

I couldn't wait to go see Gry and talk with her
about the visit. I had been kept close to the house while
we waited on Ogge's whim, but usually I was free to go
where I pleased, once the work was done; so in the afternoon of the next day, I told my mother I was riding
over to Roddmant. She looked at me with her clear
eyes, and I blushed, but she said nothing. I asked my father if I could take the red colt. I felt an unusual assur-
ance as I spoke to him. He had seen me show the gift
of our lineage, and heard me spoken of as a potential

bridegroom. It didn't surprise me when he said I could ride the colt, without reminding me to keep him from shying at cattle and to walk him after I let him run, as he would have reminded me when I was a boy of thirteen, instead of a man of thirteen.

✦ 7 ✦

I set off, like any man, full of cares and self-importance. The colt Branty had lovely, springy gaits. On the open slopes of Long Meadows, his canter was a dipping flow like a bird's flight. He ignored the staring cattle; he behaved perfectly, as if he too respected my new authority. I was pleased with both of us as we came, still at a canter, to the Stone House of Roddmant. A girl ran in to tell Gry I had come, while I walked Branty slowly round the courtyard to cool him off. He was such a tall, grand-looking horse, he made the person with him feel grand and admirable too. I strutted like a peacock as Gry came running across the yard to greet us with delight. The colt of course responded to her gift: he looked at her with great interest, ears forward, took a step towards her, bowed his head a little, and pushed his big forehead up against hers. She received the salutation gravely, rubbed his topknot, blew gently into his nostrils, and talked to him with the soft noises she called creature talk. To me she said nothing, but her smile was bright.

"When he's cooled off, let's go to the waterfall," I said, and so when Branty had been established in a stall in the stable with a bit of hay and a handful of oats, Gry and I set off up the glen. A mile or so up the mill creek the two feeders came together in a dark, narrow cleft, and leapt down from boulder to boulder to a deep pool. Cool, ceaseless wind from the falling water kept the wild azalea and black willow bushes nodding. Among them a little bird that sang a three-note song was always hidden, and an ouzel nested by the lower pool. As soon as we got there we went wading, and then ducked under the falls, and climbed the rocks, and swam and scrambled and shouted, and finally clambered up to a high, broad ledge that jutted into the sunlight. There we stretched out to get dry. It was a day of early spring, not very warm, and the water had been icy, but we were like otters, never really feeling the cold.

We had no name for that ledge, but it had been our talking place for years now.

For a while we lay and panted and soaked up the sunlight. But I was full of what I had to say, and soon enough began to say it. "Brantor Ogge Drum called on us yesterday," I informed Gry.

"I saw him once," she said. "When Mother took me on a hunt there. He looks like he'd swallowed a barrel."

"He's a powerful man," I said stuffily. I wanted her to recognise Ogge's grandeur, so that she would give me due credit for sacrificing my chance to become his son-in-law. But after all, I hadn't yet told her about that. Now that it was time to tell her, I found it difficult.

We lay on our bellies on the warm, smooth rock, like two skinny lizards. Our heads were close together so that we could speak quietly, as Gry liked to do. She was not secretive, and could yell like a wildcat, but she liked talk to be soft.

"He invited us to Drummant in May."

No response.

"He said he wanted me to meet his granddaughter. She's a Caspro through her mother." I heard the echo of my father's voice in mine.

Gry made an indistinct sound and said nothing for a long time. Her eyes were shut. Her damp hair was tangled over the side of her face that I could see; the other side was pillowed on the rock. I thought she was going to sleep.

"Are you going to?" she murmured.

"Meet his granddaughter? Of course."

"Be betrothed," she said, still with her eyes shut.

"No!" I said, indignant but uncertain.

"Are you sure?"

After a pause I said, "Yes," with less indignation, but no more certainty.

"Mother wants to betroth me," Gry said. She turned her head so that she was looking straight before her, with her chin resting on the stone.

"To Annren Barre of Cordemant," I said, pleased with myself for knowing this. It did not please Gry. She hated to know that anyone talked about her. She wanted to live invisibly, like the bird in the black willows. She said nothing at all, and I felt foolish. I said by way of apology, "My father and your father have talked about it." Still she said nothing. She had asked me, why shouldn't I ask her? But it was hard to. Finally I forced myself. "Are you going to?"

"I don't know," she muttered through closed teeth, her chin on the stone, her gaze straight ahead.

A fine reward, I thought, for my saying no so staunchly to her question. I was ready to give up Drum's granddaughter for Gry, but Gry wasn't willing to give up this Annren Barre for me? That hurt me sorely. I broke out, "I always thought—" Then I stopped.

"So did I," Gry murmured. And after a while, so softly her words were almost lost in the noise of the falls, "I told Mother I wouldn't be betrothed till I was fifteen. To anybody. Father agreed. She's angry."

She suddenly turned over onto her back and lay gazing up into the sky. I did the same. Our hands were close, lying on the rock, but did not touch.

"When you're fifteen," I said.

"When we're fifteen," she said.

That was all we said for a long time.

I lay in the sun and felt happiness like the sunlight shining through me, like the strength of the rock under me.

"Call the bird," I murmured.

She whistled three notes, and from the nodding thickets below us came the sweet, prompt reply. After a minute the bird called again, but Gry did not answer.

She could have called the bird to her hand, to perch on her finger, but she did not. When she began to come into her full power, last year, we used to play all kinds of games with her gift. She would have me wait in a clearing in the woods, not knowing what I was to see, watching with the hunter's strained alertness, till all at once, always startling me, a doe and her fawns would be standing at the edge of the clearing. Or I'd smell fox and look all about till I saw the fox sitting in the grass not six feet from me, demure as a house cat, his tail curled elegantly round his paws. Once I smelled some rank odor that made the hair stand up on my head and arms, and saw a brown bear come across the clearing, heavy-footed, soft-footed, without a glance at me, and vanish into the forest. Gry would slip into the clearing presently, smiling shyly— "Did you like that?" In the case of the bear, I admitted that I thought one was enough. She said only, "He lives on the west spur of Mount Airn. He followed the Spate down here, fishing."

She could call a hawk down off the wind, or bring the trout of the waterfall pool up to leap in air. She could guide a swarm of bees wherever the beekeeper wanted them. Once, in a mischievous mood, she kept a cloud of gnats pursuing a shepherd all across the boglands below Red Cairn. Hidden up in the cairn, watching the poor fellow's swats and starts and windmilling arms and mad rushes to escape, we snorted and wept with heartless laughter.

But we had been children then.

Now, as we lay side by side gazing up at the bright sky and the sprays of restless leaves that nodded across it, the warm rock under us and the warm sun on us, through my peaceful happiness crept the thought that I had come with more than one thing to tell Gry. We had spoken of betrothals. But neither I nor she had said anything about my coming into my power.

That was more than half a month ago now. I had not seen Gry in all that time, first because I had been going out with my father and Alloc to mend the sheep fences, and then because we had had to wait at home for Ogge's visit. If Ogge had heard about the adder, surely Gry had. Yet she had said nothing. And I had said nothing.

She was waiting for me to speak, I thought. And then I thought maybe she was waiting for me to show my power. To display it, as she had done so simply and easily, whistling to the bird. But I can't, I thought, all the warmth draining out of me, my peacefulness lost. I can't do it. At once I got angry, demanding, Why do I have to do it? Why do I have to kill something, ruin it, destroy it? Why is that my gift? I won't, I won't do it!— But all you have to do is untie a knot, a colder voice said in me. Have Gry tie a hard knot in a bit of ribbon, and then undo it with a glance. Anyone with the gift can do that. Alloc can do that— And the angry voice repeated, I won't, I don't want to, I won't!

I sat up and put my head in my hands.

Gry sat up beside me. She scratched at a nearly healed scab on her thin brown leg, and spread out her thin brown toes fanwise for a minute. I was deep in my own sudden fear and anger, yet was aware that she wanted to say something, that she was bringing herself to speak.

"I went with Mother to Cordemant last time," she said.

"You saw him then."

"Who?"

"That Annren."

"Oh, I've seen him before," she said, utterly dismissing that subject. "It was for a big hunt. Elk. They wanted us to bring the herd that comes down the Renny from Airnside. They had six crossbowmen. Mother wanted me to come. She wanted me to call the elk. I didn't want to. But she said I had to. She said people wouldn't believe I had the gift if I didn't use it. I said I'd rather train horses. She said anybody can train horses, but they need us to call the elk. She said, 'You can't withhold the gift from need.' So I went with the hunt. And I called the elk." She seemed to be watching the elk come pacing to her through the air, on our high perch. She gave a deep sigh. "They came... The bowmen shot five of them. Three young bulls and an old bull and a cow. Before we left they gave us a lot of meat, and presents—a cask of mead, and yarn, and woven goods. They gave me a beautiful shawl. I'll show it to you. Mother was really happy about the hunt. They gave us a knife, too. It's a beauty. It has an elkhorn handle mounted in silver. Father says it's an old war dagger. They sent it for him, as a kind of joke. Hanno Corde said, 'You give to our need, we give to your not-need!' But Father likes it." Hugging her knees, she sighed again, not unhappily, yet as if something oppressed her.

I didn't know why she had told me the story. Not that she needed a particular reason; we told each other everything that happened to us, everything we thought. She was not boasting; she never boasted. I did not know what the elk hunt had meant to her, if she was happy about it or proud of it or not. Maybe she didn't know herself, and told the story to find out. Maybe by telling it she was asking for my story, my triumph. But I could not tell it.

"When you call," I said, and stopped.

She waited.

"What does it feel like?"

"I don't know." She didn't understand my question; I hardly did myself.

"The first time your gift worked," I said, trying another tack, "did you know it was working? Was it sort of different from, from the times it didn't work?"

"Oh," she said. "Yes." But nothing more.

I waited.

"It just works," she said. She frowned, and wriggled her toes, and thought, and finally said, "It's different from your gift, Orrec. You have to use the eye, and…"

She hesitated and I filled in, "Eye, hand, word, will."

"Yes. But with calling, you just have to find where the creature is, and think about it, and of course it's different with each one, but it's just sort of like reaching out, or like calling aloud, only you don't use your hand, or your voice, mostly."

"But you know when it's working."

"Yes. Because they're there. You know where they are. You feel it. And they answer. Or they come…It's like a line between you and them. A cord, a string, from here," and she touched her breastbone, "between you and them. Stretched. Like a string on a fiddle—you know? If you just touch it, it calls out?" I must have looked blank. She shook her head. "It's hard to talk about!"

"But you know you're doing it, when you do it."

"Oh yes. Even before I could call, sometimes I could feel the string. Only it wasn't stretched enough. It wasn't tuned."

I sat hunched up, despairing. I tried to say something about the adder. No words would come.

Gry said, "What was it like when you killed the adder?"

So simply, she gave me my release from silence.

I could not accept it. I started to speak, and broke into tears. Only for a moment. The tears made me angry, shamed me. "It wasn't like anything," I said. "It was just—just nothing. Easy. Everybody makes this fuss about it. It's stupid!"

I stood up and walked right to the end of the ledge of rock, put my hands on my knees and stooped far over to look down to the pool below the falls. I wanted to do something daring, courageous, foolhardy. "Come on!" I said, turning. "Race you to the pool!" Gry was up and off the rock quick as a squirrel. I won the race, but skinned both knees doing it.

• • •

I RODE BRANTY HOME over the sunlit hills, and walked him to cool him down, toweled him and brushed him, watered him and fed him, left him whuffling at Roanie in his stall, and came in conscious of having fulfilled my responsibilities, as a man should do. My father said nothing, and that too was as it should be: he took it for granted that I had done what should be done. After supper Mother told us a story from the *Chamhan*, the saga of the Bendraman people, which she knew pretty well from beginning to end. She told of the hero Hamneda's raid on the demon city, his defeat by the demon king, his flight into the wasteland. My father listened as intently as I did. I remember that evening as the last—the last of the good days? the last of my childhood? I don't know what came to an end there, but I woke next morning into a different world.

"Come out with me, Orrec," my father said late in

the morning, and I thought he meant we would ride together, but he only walked with me some way towards the ash grove, till we were out of sight of the house, in the lonely, grassy swale of the Ashbrook. He said nothing as we walked. He stopped on the hillside above the brook. "Show me your gift, Orrec," he said.

I've said that obedience to my father had always been a pleasure to me, though often not an easy pleasure. And it was a very deep habit, a lifelong, unbroken custom. I had simply never thought of disobeying him, never wanted to. What he asked of me, even if difficult, was always possible, and even if incomprehensible, always turned out to be reasonable, to be right. I understood what he was asking of me now, and why he asked it. But I would not do it.

A flint stone and a steel blade may lie side by side for years, quiet as can be, but strike them together and the spark leaps. Rebellion is an instant thing, immediate, a spark, a fire.

I stood facing him, the way I always stood when he spoke my name that way, and said nothing.

He gestured to a ragged clump of grasses and bindweed near us. "Unmake that," he said, his tone not commanding but encouraging.

I stood still. After one glance at the clump of weeds, I did not look back at it.

He waited some while. He drew breath, and there was some slight change in his stance, an increase of tension, though he still said nothing.

"Will you do it?" he said at last, very softly.

"No," I said.

Silence between us again. I heard the faint music of the brook and a bird singing away over in the ash grove and a cow lowing down in the home pasture.

"Can you do it?"

"I won't."

Silence again, and then he said, "There's nothing to fear, Orrec." His voice was gentle. I bit my lip and clenched my hands.

"I'm not afraid," I said.

"To control your gift you must use it," Canoc said, still with that gentleness that weakened my resolve.

"I won't use it."

"Then it may use you."

That was unexpected. What had Gry told me about using her gift and being used by it? I could not remember now. I was confused, but I would not admit it.

I shook my head.

Then at last he frowned. His head went back as if he faced an opponent. When he spoke, the tenderness had gone out of his voice. "You must show your gift, Orrec," he said. "If not to me, to others. It's not your choice to make. To have the power is to serve the power. You'll be Brantor of Caspromant. The people here will depend on you as they do on me now. You must show them they can rely on you. And learn how to use your gift by using it."

I shook my head.

After another unbearable silence, he said, almost in a whisper, "Is it the killing?"

I didn't know whether it was that, the idea that my gift was to kill, to destroy, that I rebelled against. I had thought that, but not very clearly, though I had often thought with sick horror of the rat, the adder.... All I knew by now was that I refused to be tested, refused to try out this terrible power, refused to let it be what I was. But Canoc had given me an out, and I took it. I nodded.

At that he gave a deep sigh, his only sign of disappointment or impatience, and turned away. Then he fished in his coat pocket and brought out a bit of lacing. He always carried ends of cord for all the thousand uses of a farmstead. He knotted it and tossed it onto the ground between us. He said nothing, but looked at it and at me.

"I'm not a dog, to do tricks for you!" I burst out in a shrill, loud voice. It left an awful, ringing silence between us.

"Listen, Orrec," he said. "At Drummant, that's what you'll be, if you choose to see it that way. If you don't show your gift there, what will Ogge think, and say? If you refuse to learn the use of your power, our people will have no one to turn to." He took a deep breath, and for a moment his voice shook with anger. "Do you think I like killing rats? Am I a terrier?" He stopped, and looked aside, and finally said, "Think of your duty. Of our duty. Think of it, and when you've understood it, come to me."

He stooped and picked up the length of cord, unknotted it with his fingers, put it back in his pocket, and strode away, uphill, towards the ash grove.

When I remember that now, I think of how he saved that bit of lacing, because cord was hard to come by and must not be wasted, and I could cry again; but not with the tears of shame and fury that I wept as I went down the stream valley from that place, that day.

❖ 8 ❖

After that nothing could be the same between my father and me, because now there lay between us his demand and my refusal. But his manner to me did not change. He did not return to the matter for several days. When he did it was not to command but to ask almost casually, one afternoon when we were riding back from our eastern boundary: "Are you ready to try your power now?"

But my determination had grown up round me like a wall, a stone tower-keep in which I was protected from his demands, his questions, my own questions. I answered at once: "No."

My flat certainty must have taken him aback. He said nothing in reply. He said nothing to me as we rode on home. He said nothing to me the rest of that day. He looked tired and stern. My mother saw that, and probably guessed the cause.

The next morning she asked me to come up to her room on the pretext of fitting the coat she was making for me. While she had me standing with my arms stuck out like a straw doll and was going round me on her knees taking out basting stitches and marking button-holes, she said through the pins in her mouth, "Your father's worried."

I scowled and said nothing.

She took the pins out of her mouth and sat back on her heels. "He says he doesn't know why Brantor Ogge acted as he did. Inviting himself here, and inviting us there, and dropping hints about his granddaughter, and all. He says there's never been any friendship between Drum and Caspro. I said, 'Well, better late than never.' But he just shakes his head. It worries him."

This was not what I'd expected, and it drew me from my self-absorption. I didn't know what to say but sought for something wise and reassuring. "Maybe it's because our domains border now," was the best I could come up with.

"I think that's what worries him," Melle said. She replaced one pin between her lips and set another in the hem of the jacket. It was a man's coat of black felt, my first.

"So," she said, removing the pin from her mouth and sitting back again to judge the fit, "I'll be very glad when this visit's over with!"

I felt guilt weigh me down, as if the black coat were made of lead.

"Mother," I said, "he wants me to practice the gift, the undoing, and I don't want to, and it makes him angry."

"I know," she said. She went on adjusting the hang of the jacket, and then stopped and looked at me, up at me, because she was kneeling and I standing. "That's something I can't help either of you with. You see that, don't you, Orrec? I don't understand it. I can't meddle in it. I can't come between you and your father, either. It's hard, when I see you both unhappy. All I can say to you is, it's for you, for all of us, that he asks this of you. He wouldn't ask it if it were wrong. You know that."

She had to take his part and his side, of course. It was right, and just, but also it was unfair, unfair to me, that all the power should be on his side, all the right, all the reasons, that even she had to be on his side—leaving me alone, a stupid, stubborn boy, unable to use my power, claim my right, or speak my reasons. Because I saw that unfairness, I would not even try to speak. I drew away, into my furious shame, my stone tower, and stood mute inside it.

"Is it because you don't want to harm creatures that you don't want to use your power, Orrec?" she asked, quite timidly. Even with me she was timid, humble before this uncanny gift she knew so little of.

But I would not answer her question. I did not nod or shrug or speak. She glanced into my face, then looked back at her work and finished it in silence. She slipped the half-made jacket off my shoulders, held me briefly to her, kissed my cheek, and let me go.

Twice after that, Canoc asked me if I would try my gift. Twice I silently refused. The third time he did not ask, but said, "Orrec, you must obey me now."

I stood silent. We were not far from the house, but no one else was around. He never tested or shamed me before other people.

"Tell me what you're afraid of."

I stood silent.

He faced me, close to me, his eyes blazing, so much pain and passion in his voice that it struck me like the lash of a whip: "Are you afraid of your power or afraid you don't have the power?"

I caught my breath and cried out, "I am not afraid!"

"Then use your gift! Now! Strike anything!" He flung out his right hand. His left was clenched and held to his side.

"No!" I said, shaking and shivering, holding both my clenched hands to my chest, ducking my head because I could not stand the blaze of his eyes.

I heard him turn and go. His steps went down the path and into the courtyard of the house. I did not look up. I stood staring and staring at a little clump of broom just leafing out in the April sunlight. I stared at it and thought of it black, dead, withered, but I did not lift my hand, or use my voice or my will. I only stared at it and saw it green, alive, indifferent.

After that he did not ask me again to use my power. Everything went on as usual. He spoke to me much as usual. He did not smile or laugh, and I could not look into his face.

I went to see Gry when I could, riding Roanie because I didn't want to ask if I could ride the colt. A hound bitch at Roddmant had whelped a monstrous litter of pups, fourteen of them; they were well past the weaning stage, but still very funny and foolish, and we played with them a good deal. I was making much of one of them when Ternoc stopped by to watch us. "Here, take the pup," he said, "take it home with you. We could use a few less, to be sure, and Canoc said he might be wanting a hound or two. That's a likely young dog, I'd say." He was the prettiest of the lot, pure black and tan. I was delighted.

"Take Biggie," Gry said. "He's a lot smarter."

"But I like this one. He's always kissing me." The puppy obliged, washing my face quite thoroughly.

"Kissie," Gry said, without enthusiasm.

"No, he's not Kissie! He's…" I sought a heroic name and found it. "He's Hamneda."

Gry looked dubious and uneasy, but she never argued. So I carried the long-legged black-and-tan puppy home in a basket on the saddle, and for a little while he was my solace and playmate. But of course I should have heeded Gry, who knew her dogs as no one else could know them. Hamneda was hopelessly backward and excitable. He not only pissed on the floor like any puppy, but soiled anywhere and everywhere, so that he soon had to be forbidden the house; he hurt himself, got between the horses' feet, killed our best stable

mouser and her kittens, bit the gardener and the cook's
little boy, and exasperated everyone with the meaningless, shrill barking and whining he kept up day and
night, which grew even worse when he was shut up
to keep him out of trouble. He could not learn to do,
or not do, anything at all. I was sick to death of him
after a halfmonth. I wished I was rid of him, but was
ashamed to admit, even to myself, my disloyalty to the
hapless, brainless dog.

Alloc and I were to ride with my father one morning up to the high pastures to check on the spring calv-
ing there. As usual my father rode Greylag, but this
time he told Alloc to take Roanie while I rode the colt.
That was a dubious privilege, this morning. Branty was
in a vile temper. He tossed his head, he held his breath,
he kicked out and tried to bite, he bucked when I
mounted, he sidled and backed and embarrassed me in
every way. Just as I thought I had him under control,
Hamneda burst out from somewhere and came leaping
straight at the colt, yapping, a broken leash flailing all
about him. I yelled at the dog as Branty reared right up,
unseating me. I managed not to fall, and to regain my
seat, and to rein the scared colt in, all in a wild flurry.
When Branty finally stood still, I looked for the dog

and saw a heap of black and tan on the courtyard
pavement.

"What happened?" I said.

My father, sitting his horse, looked at me. "Do you
not know?"

I stared at Hamneda. I thought Branty must have
trampled him. But there was no blood. He lay boneless,
shapeless. One long black-and-tan leg lay like limp
rope. I swung off the horse, but I could not go nearer
that thing lying on the pavement.

I stared up at my father and cried out, "Did you
have to kill him?"

"Was it I?" Canoc said, in a voice that turned me
cold.

"Ah, Orrec, it was you," said Alloc, bringing Roanie
over closer—"sure enough, you flung out your hand,
you were saving the horse from the fool of a dog!"

"I did not!" I said. "I did—I did not kill him!"

"Do you know whether you did or not?" Canoc
said, almost jeering, it seemed.

"It was just as when you destroyed the adder, sure
enough," Alloc said. "A quick eye!" But his voice was a
little uneasy or unhappy. People had come into the
courtyard from the house and outside, hearing the com-

motion, and stood staring. The horses fretted, wanting to stand away from the dead dog. Branty, whom I held close at the bridle, was shivering and sweating, and so was I. All at once I turned away and vomited, but I did not let go the reins. When I had wiped my mouth and got my breath, I led Branty to the mounting stone and got back up in the saddle. I could barely speak, but I said, "Are we going?"

And we rode on up to the high pastures, in silence all the way.

That evening I asked where they had buried the dog. I went to the place, out past the midden, and stood there. I could not grieve much for poor Hamneda, but there was a terrible grief in me. When I started back to the house in the late dusk, my father was on the path.

"I'm sorry about your dog, Orrec," he said in his grave, quiet voice.

I nodded.

"Tell me this: did you will to destroy him?"

"No," I said, but I did not speak with entire certainty, because nothing was clear or certain to me any more. I had hated the dog for his idiocy, for scaring the colt, but I had not wanted to kill him for it, had I?

"Yet you did."

"Without meaning to?"

"You didn't know you were using your gift?"

"No!"

He had turned to walk with me, and we went on towards the house in silence. The spring twilight was sweet and cold. The evening star hung near the young moon in the west.

"Am I like Caddard?" I asked in a whisper.

He took a long time to answer. "You must try to learn the use of the gift, to control it," he said.

"But I can't. Nothing happens when I try to use it, Father! I've tried and tried— It's only when I don't try— when it's something like the adder—or today—and it doesn't seem like I do anything—it just happens—"

The words all came at once, the stones of my towerkeep clattering down around me.

Canoc did not reply except with a little sound of compunction. He put his hand lightly on my shoulder as we walked. As we came to the gate, he said, "There is what they call the wild gift."

"Wild?"

"A gift not controlled by the will."

"Is it dangerous?"

He nodded.

"What do—what do you do about it?"

"Have patience," he said, and again his hand was on my shoulder for a moment. "Take courage, Orrec. We'll find out what we must do."

It was a relief to know my father was not angry with me, and to be free of that furious resistance to him in myself; but what he had said was frightening enough to leave me little comfort that night. When in the morning he summoned me to go with him, I came readily. If there was something I could do, I would do it.

He was silent and stern that morning. I thought it was all to do with me, of course, but he said as we walked towards the Ashbrook vale: "Dorec came this morning. He says two of the white heifers are missing."

The heifers were of the old Rodd stock, three beautiful creatures, for which Canoc had traded a big piece of good woodland on our border with Roddmant. He was hoping to build up a herd of those cattle again at Caspromant. The three had been pastured this last month in a bit of fat grassland at the south edge of the domain, near the sheep grazings. A serf woman and her son whose cottage was near that pasture kept an eye on them along with the five or six milch cows she kept there.

"Did they find a break in the fences?" I asked.

He shook his head.

The heifers were the most valuable thing we had, aside from Greylag, Roanie, and Branty, and the land itself. The loss of two of them would be a hard blow to Canoc's hopes.

"Are we going to go look for them?"

He nodded. "Today."

"They might have got up onto the Sheer—"

"Not by themselves," he said.

"Do you think…." I did not go on. If the heifers had been stolen, there were all too many likely thieves. The likeliest, in that part of the domain, would be Drum or some of his people. But speculation about cattle thieving was a risky thing. Murderous feuds had been started over a careless word, not even an accusation. Though my father and I were alone, the habit of discretion in these matters was strong. We said nothing more.

We came to the same spot we had stopped at days ago, when I first defied him. He said, "Will you—" and stopped, completing his question with an almost pleading look at me. I nodded.

I looked about. The hillside rose gently up, grassy and stony, hiding the higher slopes above it. A little ash tree had got a foothold near the path and was struggling to grow there by itself, spindly and dwarfed, but putting out its leaf buds bravely. I looked away from it. There was an ant hill by the path ahead of us. It was early morning yet, and the big, reddish-black ants were still boiling in and out of the opening at the top, forming lines, hurrying along on their business. It was a large hill, a mound of bare clay standing a foot tall. I had seen the ruins of such insect cities and could imagine the tunnels underground, the complex galleries and passages, the dark architecture. In that instant, not giving myself time to think, I stretched out my left hand and stared at the ant hill and the breath burst from my lips in a sharp sound as I struck with all my will to unmake, undo, destroy it.

I saw the green grass in the sunlight, the dwarf ash tree, the bare brown ant hill, the reddish-black ants hurrying in and out of its narrow mouth, going and coming in straggling columns through the grass and across the path.

My father was standing behind me. I did not turn around. I heard his silence. I could not bear it.

In a passion of frustration, I shut my eyes tight, wishing I need never see this place again, the ants, the grass, the path, the sunlight—

I opened my eyes and saw the grass curl and turn

black, the ants stop and shrivel up into nothing, their hill collapsing into dusty caverns. The ground seemed to writhe and boil before me up the hillside with a cracking, splitting rattle, and something that stood before me shuddered and twisted and turned black. My left hand was still out stiff, pointing before me. I clenched it, brought both hands up over my face. "Stop it! Stop it!" I shouted.

My father's hands were on my shoulders. He held me against him. "There," he said, "there. It's done, Orrec. It's done." I could feel that he was shaking, as I was, and his breath came short.

When I took my hands away from my eyes, I turned my head away at once, terrified by what I saw. Half the hillside before us was as if a whirlwind of fire had swept across it—ruined, withered—a litter of split pebbles on dead ground. The ash tree was a split black stump.

I turned around and hid my face against my father's chest. "I thought it was you, I thought it was you standing there!"

"What is it, son?" He was very gentle, keeping his hands on me as he would with a scared foal, talking quietly.

"I would have killed you!—But I didn't, I didn't mean to! I didn't *do* it! I did it but I didn't will it! What can I do!"

"Listen, listen, Orrec. Don't be afraid. I won't ask you again—"

"But it's no use! I can't control it! I can't do it when I want to do it and then when I don't want to do it I do! I don't dare look at you! I don't dare look at anything! What if I—what if I—" But I couldn't go on. I sank right down on the ground paralysed by terror and despair.

Canoc sat down on the dirt of the path beside me and let me recover myself by myself.

I sat up at last. I said, "I am like Caddard."

It was a statement and a question.

"Maybe—" my father said, "maybe like Caddard was as a child. Not as he was when he killed his wife. He was mad then. But as a young child, it was his gift that was wild. It wasn't under his control."

I said, "They blindfolded him till he learned how to control it. You could blindfold me."

After I said it, it seemed a crazy thing, and I wanted it unsaid. But I raised my head and looked at the hillside in front of me, a broad swathe of dead grass and withered shrubs, dust and shattered stones, a formless ruin. Any living thing that had been there was dead. All the delicate, coherent, complex shapes of the things that had been there were destroyed. The ash tree was a hideous, branchless stump. I had done that and not known I was doing it. I had not willed to do it, yet I had done it. I had been angry...

I shut my eyes once more. "It would be best," I said.

Perhaps there was some hope in me that my father would have a different, a better plan. But, after a long time, and in a low voice as if ashamed that it was all he could say, he said, "Maybe for a while."

❖ 9 ❖

Neither of us was ready to do what we had spoken of doing or even to think about it yet. There was the matter of the heifers, strayed or stolen. Of course I wanted to ride with him to look for them, and he wanted me with him. So we went back to the Stone House and mounted, along with Alloc and a couple of other young men, and were off without another word about what had happened beside the Ashbrook.

But all that long day from time to time I would look at the green vales, the willows along the streams, the heather in blossom and the early yellow broom flowers, and up to the blue and brown of the great hills, scanning for the heifers, but at the same time afraid of looking, afraid of staring too hard, of seeing the grass blacken and the trees wither in an invisible flame. Then I would look away, look down, clench my left hand to my side, close my eyes a moment, try to think of nothing, see nothing.

It was a weary day, fruitless. The old woman who had been charged with guarding the heifers was so terrified of Canoc's anger that she couldn't say anything that made sense. Her son, who should have been watching over them in the pasture near Drummant land, had been up on the mountain hunting hares. We found no break in the fences where the cattle might have got through, but they were old stone fences with palings along the top which could have been easily pulled out and replaced by thieves covering their tracks. Or the heifers, still young and adventurous, might have simply wandered off up one of the glens and be peacefully grazing away somewhere on the vast, folded slopes of the East Sheer. But in that case, it was odd that one of them had stayed behind. Cattle follow one another. The one pretty young cow left, shut up now, too late, in the barnyard, mooed mournfully from time to time, calling her friends.

Alloc and his cousin Dorec and the old woman's son were left to search the high slopes, while my father and I rode home a roundabout way that took us clear up along our border with Drummant, keeping an eye out for white cattle all the way. Now, as I rode, whenever we were on high ground I stretched my gaze westward looking for the heifers, and thought what it would be like not to be able to do that: not to be able to look: to see only blackness no matter how I looked. What good would I be then? Instead of helping my father, I would be a burden to him. That thought was hard. I began thinking of things that I would not be able to do, and from that began thinking of things that I would not be able to see, thinking of them one by one: this hill, that tree. The round grey crest of Mount Airn. The cloud over it. The twilight gathering round the Stone House as we rode down the glen towards it. Dim yellow light in a window. Roanie's ears in front of me, turning and flicking. Branty's dark, bright eye under his red forelock. My mother's face. The little opal she wore on a silver chain. I saw and thought of each separate thing, each time with a sharp piercing pain, because all those little pangs, though they were endless, were still easier to bear than the single immense pain of realising that I must not see anything, that I must see nothing, that I must be blind.

We were both very tired, and I thought perhaps we'd go on saying nothing at least for one more night, that Canoc would put it off till morning (and what would morning mean, when I could not see the light above the hills?). But after our supper, eaten in weary silence, he said to my mother that we must talk, and we went up to her tower room, where a fire was laid. It had been a bright day but a cool one, the windy end of April, and the night was cold. The warmth of the fire was very pleasant on my legs and face. I will feel that when I can't see it, I thought.

My father and mother were speaking of the lost heifers. I gazed into the fire as it caught and flared, and the weary peacefulness that had taken hold of me for a minute slipped away. Little by little my heart filled up with an immense anger at the injustice of what had befallen me. I would not bear it, I would not endure it. I would not blind myself because my father feared me! The fire leapt up along a dry branch, crackling and sparking, and I caught my breath, turning towards them, towards him.

He sat in the wooden chair. My mother sat on the

cross-legged stool she liked, beside him; her hand lay on his, on his knee. Their faces in the firelight were shadowed, tender, mysterious. My left hand was raised, pointing at him, trembling. I saw that, and I saw the ash tree on the hillside above the brook writhe and its branches blacken, and I clapped both my hands up over my eyes, hard, pressing hard, so I could not see, so I could not see anything but the blurs of color in blackness that you see when you press hard on your eyes.

"What is it, Orrec?" My mother's voice.

"Tell her, Father!"

Hesitantly, laboriously, he began to tell her what had happened. He did not tell it in order, or clearly, and I grew impatient with his clumsiness. "Say what happened to Hamneda, tell what happened by the Ashbrook!" I commanded, pressing my hands to my eyes, closing them tighter, as the awful anger swept through me again. Why couldn't he just say it? He mixed it up and began again and seemed unable to come to the point, to say what it all led to. My mother barely spoke, trying to make sense of all this confusion and distress. "But this wild gift—?" she asked finally, and when Canoc hesitated again, I broke in: "What it means is, I have the power of unmaking but I haven't any power over it. I can't use it when I want to and then I do use it when I don't want to. I could kill you both if I looked at you right now."

There was a silence, and then she said, resisting, indignant, "But surely—"

"No," my father said. "Orrec is telling the truth."

"But you've trained him, taught him, for years, ever since he was a baby!"

Her protests only sharpened my pain and rage. "It wasn't any use," I said. "I'm like the dog. Hamneda. He couldn't learn. He was useless. And dangerous. The best thing to do was kill him."

"Orrec!"

"The power itself," Canoc said, "not Orrec, but his power—his gift. He can't use it, and it may use him. It's dangerous, as he says. To him, to us, to everyone. In time he'll learn to control it. It is a great gift, he's young, in time…But for now, for now it has to be taken from him."

"How?" Mother's voice was a thread.

"A blindfold."

"A blindfold!"

"The sealed eye has no power."

"But a blindfold— You mean, when he's outside the house— When he's with other people—"

"No," Canoc said, and I said, "No. All the time. Until I know I'm not going to hurt somebody or kill somebody without even knowing I'm doing it till it's done, till they're dead, till they're lying there like a bag of meat. I won't do that again. Ever again. Ever." I sat there by the hearth with my hands pressed to my eyes, hunched up, sick, sick and dizzy in that blackness. "Seal my eyes now," I said. "Do it now."

If Melle protested and Canoc insisted further, I don't remember. I only remember my own agony. And the relief at last, when my father came to me where I sat crouching there by the hearth, and gently took my hands down from my face, slipped a cloth over my eyes, and tied it at the back of my head. It was black, I saw it before he tied it on me, the last thing I saw: firelight, and a strip of black cloth in my father's hands.

Then I had darkness.

And I felt the warmth of the unseen fire, as I had imagined I would.

My mother was crying, quietly, trying not to let me hear her cry; but the blind have keen ears. I had no desire to weep. I had shed enough tears. I was very tired. Their voices murmured. The fire crackled softly. Through the warm darkness I heard my mother say, "He's falling asleep," and I was.

My father must have carried me to my bed like a little child.

When I woke it was dark, and I sat up to see if there was any hint of dawn over the hills out my window, and could not see the window, and wondered if heavy clouds had come in and hidden the stars. Then I heard the birds singing for sunrise, and put my hands up to the blindfold.

* * *

IT'S A QUEER business, making oneself blind. I had asked Canoc what the will was, what it meant to will something. Now I learned what it meant.

To cheat, to look, one glance, only a glance—the temptations of course were endless. Every step, every act that was now so immensely difficult and complicated and awkward could become easy and natural so easily and naturally. Just lift the blindfold, just for a moment, just from one eye, just take one peek. . . .

I did not lift the blindfold, but it did slip several times, and my eyes would dazzle with all the brightness of the world's day before I could close them. We learned to lay soft patches over the eyelids before tying the cloth round my head; then it did not need to be tied so painfully tight. And I was safe from sight.

That is how I felt: safe. Learning to be blind was a queer business, yes, and a hard one, but I kept to it. The more impatient I was with the helplessness and dreariness of being sightless and the more I raged against the blindfold, the more I feared to lift it. It saved me from the horror of destroying what I did not mean to destroy. While I wore it, I could not kill what I loved. I remembered what my fear and anger had done. I remembered the moment when I thought I had destroyed my father. If I could not learn to use my power, I could learn how not to use it.

That was what I willed to do, because only so could my will act. Only in this bondage could I have any freedom.

On the first day of my blindness, I groped my way down to the entrance hall of the Stone House and felt along the wall till my hands found Blind Caddard's staff. I had not looked at it for years. My childish game of touching it because I wasn't supposed to touch it had been half my life ago. But I remembered where it was, and I knew I had a right to it now.

It was too tall for me and awkwardly heavy, but I liked the worn, silken feeling of the place where I grasped it, a little higher than I would naturally have reached. I stuck it out, swept it across the floor, knocked the end of it against the wall. It guided me back across the hall. After that I often carried it when I went outside. Inside the house I did better using my hands to feel my way. Outdoors, the staff gave me a certain reassurance. It was a weapon. If I was threatened, I could strike with it. Not strike with the hideous power of my gift, but a straight blow, simple retaliation and defense. Sightless, I felt forever vulnerable, knowing that anybody could make a fool of me or hurt me. The heavy stick in my hand made up for that, a little.

At first my mother was not the comfort to me she had always been. It was to my father that I turned for unwavering approval and support. Mother could not approve, could not believe that what I was doing was right and necessary. To her it was monstrous, the result of monstrous, unnatural powers or beliefs. "You can take off the blindfold when you're with me, Orrec," she said.

"Mother, I can't."

"It is silly to be afraid, Orrec. It's foolish. You'll never hurt me. I know that. Wear it outside if you have to, but not in here with me. I want to see your eyes, my son!"

"Mother, I can't." That was all I could say. I had to say it again and again, for she cajoled and persuaded.

She had not seen Hamneda's death; she had never gone out along the Ashbrook to see that ghastly, blasted hillside. I thought of asking her to go there, but could not. I would not answer her arguments.

At last she spoke to me with real bitterness. "This is ignorant superstition, Orrec," she said. "I am ashamed of you. I thought I had taught you better. Do you think a rag around your eyes will keep you from doing evil, if there's evil in your heart? And if there's good in your heart, how will you do good now? 'Will you stop the wind with a wall of grasses, or the tide by telling it to stay?'" In her despair she returned to the liturgies of Bendraman that she had learned as a child in her father's house.

And when I still held firm, she said, "Shall I burn the book I made you, then? It's no use to you now. You don't want it. You've closed your eyes—you've closed your mind."

That made me cry out—"It's not forever, Mother!" I did not like to speak or think of any term to my blindness, of a day when I might see again: I dared not imagine it, because I could not imagine what would allow it, and feared false hope. But her threat, and her pain, wrung it out of me.

"How long, then?"

"I don't know. Until I learn—" But I didn't know what to say. How was I to learn to use a gift I couldn't use? Hadn't I been trying to, all my life?

"You've learned all your father could teach you," she said. "Learned it only too well." She stood up then and left me without another word. I heard the soft swish as she threw her shawl over her shoulders, and her steps going out of the hall.

She was not of the unyielding temper that could hold such anger long. That night as we said goodnight I could hear in her voice her sweet rueful smile as she whispered, "I won't burn your book, dear son. Or your blindfold." And from then on she did not plead and made no more protest, but took my blindness as a fact and helped me as she could.

The best way I found to be blind was to try to act as if I could see: not to creep and feel my way about, but to step out, knock my face against the wall if I met a wall, and fall if I fell. I learned my ways about the house and yards and kept to them, but used them freely, going outdoors as often as I could. I saddled and bridled good Roanie, who was patient with my fumbling as she had been patient with it when I was five, and mounted her and let her take me where she thought best. Once in the saddle and out of the echoes of the walls of the stable yard, there was nothing to guide me at all; I might be on the hillsides or the highlands or the moon for all I knew. But Roanie knew where we were, and also knew I was not the thoughtless, fearless rider I had been. She looked after me, and brought me home.

"I want to go to Roddmant," I said, after my eyes had been sealed a halfmonth or longer. "I want to ask Gry to give me a dog." I had to get up my determination to say that, for poor Hamneda and the horrible thing I had made of him were in my mind as if branded into it. But the thought of having a dog to aid my blindness had come to me the night before, and I knew it was a good one. And I longed to talk with Gry.

"A dog," Canoc said with surprise, but Melle understood at once, and said, "That's a good idea. I'll ride—" I knew she had been about to say she would ride to Roddmant on my errand (though she was not much of a horsewoman, and timid even with Roanie), but what she said was, "I'll ride with you, if you like."

"Can we go tomorrow?"

"Put it off a little while," Canoc said. "It's time we were making ready to go to Drummant."

In all that had befallen me, I had utterly forgotten about Brantor Ogge and his invitation. The reminder was most unwelcome. "I can't go now!" I said.

"You can," my father said.

"Why should he? Why should we?" my mother demanded.

"I've said what's at stake." Canoc's voice was hard. "A chance of truce, if not of friendship. And the offer, maybe, of a betrothal."

"But Drum won't want to betroth his granddaughter to Orrec now!"

"Will he not? When he knows Orrec can kill at a glance? That his gift is so strong he must seal his eyes to spare his enemies? Oh, he'll be glad to ask and glad to get what we choose to give! Don't you see that?"

I had never heard that tone of harsh, fierce triumph in my father's voice. It shook me strangely. It woke me.

For the first time I realised that my blindfold made me not only vulnerable, but threatening. My power was so great that it could not be released, must be restrained. If I unsealed my eyes... I myself was, like Caddard's staff, a weapon.

And I also understood in that moment why so many of the people of the house and the domain treated me as they had done since my eyes were sealed, speaking to me with an uneasy respect instead of the old easy fellowship, falling silent as I came near, creeping past me as if they hoped I couldn't hear them. I thought they shunned and despised me because I was blind. It hadn't occurred to me that they feared me because they knew why I was blind.

Indeed, as I was to learn, the tale had grown in the telling, and I had the grisly credit of all kinds of feats. I had destroyed a whole pack of wild dogs, bursting them open like bladders. I had cleared the venomous snakes out of all Caspromant merely by sweeping my eyes over the hills. I had glanced at old Ubbro's cottage, and that same night the old man had fallen paralysed and lost the power of speech, and it was not a punishment but only the wild gift striking without reason. When I had gone looking for the missing white heifers, the instant I saw them, I had destroyed them, against my own will. And so in fear of this random and terrible power I had blinded myself—or Canoc had blinded me—though others said no, only sealed his eyes with a blindfold. If anybody disbelieved these tales, they took him to see the ruined hillside above the Ashbrook, the dead tree, the little broken bones of voles and moles and mice on the waste ground there, the burst boulders and shattered stones.

I didn't know these stories then, but it had dawned on me that I had a new power, which lay not in acts but words—in reputation.

"We'll go to Drummant," my father said. "It's time. Day after tomorrow. If we set off early we can be there by nightfall. Take your red gown, Melle. I want Drum to see the gift he gave me."

"Oh, dear," my mother said. "How long must we stay?"

"Five or six days, I suppose."

"Oh, dear, dear. What can I take the brantor's wife? I must have some guest-present for her."

"It's not necessary."

"It is," said my mother.

"Well, a basket of something from the kitchen?"

"Pah," said my mother. "There's nothing this time of year."

"A basket of chicks," I suggested. Mother had taken me into the poultry yard that morning to let me handle a brood of newly hatched chicks, putting them into my hands, cheeping, warm, weightless, downy, prickly.

"That's it," she said.

And when we set off two days later early in the morning, she had a basket full of cheeping on her saddlebow. I wore my new kilt and coat, my man's coat.

Because I must ride Roanie, she was on Greylag, who was a completely trusty horse, though his height and size scared her. My father rode the colt. He had given much of Branty's training to me and Alloc, but when you saw him ride Branty, you saw that he and the colt were made for each other, handsome, nervous, proud, and rash. I wished I could see him, that morning. I longed to see him. But I sat good Roanie and let her carry me forward into the dark.

◆ 10 ◆

It was strange and wearisome to ride all day seeing nothing of the country we rode through, aware only of the sound of hoofs on soft or stony ground, the creak of saddles, the smell of horse sweat and broom flower, the touch of the wind, guessing what the road must be like by Roanie's gait. Unable to be ready for a change, a stumble, a sway, a check, I was always tense in the saddle, and often had to abandon shame and hold the pommel to keep myself steady. Mostly we had to ride single file, so there was no conversation. We paused now and then so Mother could give the chicks water, and we stopped at midday to rest and water the horses and to eat our lunch. The chicks chirped and cheeped

vigorously over the feed Mother scattered in their basket. I asked where we were. Under Black Crag, Father
said, in the domain of the Cordes. I could not imagine
the place, never having been so far to the west of
Caspromant. We soon went on, and to me the afternoon was a dull, long, black dream.

"By the Stone!" my father said. He never swore, not
even such a mild old-fashioned oath as that, and it
startled me out of my trance. My mother was riding in
front, for there was no mistaking the path, and my father behind, keeping an eye on us. She had not heard
him speak, but I asked, "What is it?"

"Our heifers," he said, "over there." And remembering I could not see where he pointed, "There's a herd of
cattle in the meadows under the hill there, and two of
them are white. The rest are duns and roans." He was
silent a moment, probably straining his eyes to see.
"They have the hump, and the shallow horns," he said.
"It's them all right."

We had all stopped, and Mother asked, "Are we still
in Cordemant?"

"Drummant," my father said. "For the past hour.
But those are the Rodd breed. And my cows, I think. If
I got closer to them, I could be sure of it."

"Not now, Canoc," she said. "It'll be getting dark

before long. We ought to go on." There was strong apprehension in her voice. He heeded it.

"Right you are," he said, and I heard Greylag step forward, and Roanie followed him without my needing to signal her, and the colt's light step followed us.

We came to the Stone House of Drummant, and that was hard for me, that arrival in a strange place among strangers. My mother took my arm as soon as I dismounted and hung on to me, maybe to reassure herself as well as me. Among the many voices, I heard Ogge Drum's, loud and genial. "Well, well, well, so you did come at last! And welcome to you! Welcome to Drummant! We're poor folk here but what we have we share! What's this, what's this, the boy bandaged up like this? What's the trouble then, lad? Weak eyes, is it?"

"Ah, we could wish it were that," Canoc said lightly. He was a fencer; but Ogge was no swordsman, he used a bludgeon. A bully doesn't answer you; he may hear but pays no heed; he talks on as if you were of no account, and it gives him the advantage always at the start, though not always in the end.

"Well, what a shame, to be led about like a baby, but no doubt he'll grow out of it. Come this way, come this way. See to their horses, there! Barro, fetch the maids to call my lady!" and so on, a shouting of orders and commands, a great commotion, much coming and going, many voices. There were people all round me, crowds of unseen, unknown people. My mother was explaining to someone about the basket of chicks for the brantor's wife. She kept hold of my arm as I was dragged over thresholds and up stairs. My head was whirling by the time we stopped. We were brought basins of water, and people buzzed all around us as we hurriedly washed off our travel dirt and brushed our clothes and Mother changed her dress.

Then it was down stairs again, and we came into a room which, by the sound of the echoes, was a great, tall one. There was a hearth: I could hear the crackle of the fire and feel a bit of warmth on my legs and face. Mother kept her hand on my shoulder. "Orrec," she said, "here is the brantor's wife, the lady Denno," and I bowed in the direction of the hoarse, tired-sounding voice that bade me be welcome to Drummant. There followed other introductions—the brantor's elder son Harba and his wife, his younger son Sebb and his wife, his daughter and her husband, the grown children of some of these, and other people of the household—all names without faces, voices in the dark. My mother's shy, gracious voice was drowned out by these loud talkers, and I couldn't help but hear how different from them she sounded, how foreign in her Lowland courtesies, even in her pronunciation of some words.

My father was close to me too, right behind me. He didn't talk on at length the way the Drum men did, but made prompt, affable responses, laughed at their jokes, and spoke to several of the men there with what sounded like the pleasure of renewing a friendship. One of these men, a Barre, I think, said, "So the lad's got the wild eye, has he?" and Canoc said, "He does," and the other man said, "Well, never fear, he'll grow into his power," and began a story about a boy of Olmmant whose gift was wild till he was twenty. I tried hard to hear the story, but the clamor of voices kept drowning it out.

After a while we went to table, and that was a terrible strain, for it takes a long time to learn to eat in a decent fashion if you cannot see, and I had not got the skill yet. I was afraid to touch anything for fear of spilling it or soiling myself. They had tried to seat me away from my mother, and Brantor Ogge called for her to join the men at the head of the table, but she gently and immovably insisted on sitting next to me. She helped me to a chop I could pick up in my fingers and gnaw without shocking anybody's sensibilities. Not that they went in much for fine manners at Drummant, to judge by the noises of chewing and gulping and belching all round me.

My father was seated farther up the table, near or next to Ogge, and as the noise of talk slackened a bit, I heard his quiet voice, unmistakable, though there was a tone to it, a kind of lilt I'd never heard before: "I want to thank you, Brantor, for looking after my heifers. I've been cursing myself for a fool all month for not keeping my fences mended. They jumped them, of course. They're light-footed, those Rodd cattle. I'd all but given that pair up. Thought they'd be down in Dunet by now! And so they would be if your people hadn't kept them safe for me." By this time nobody at that end of the table was saying a word, though at our end some of the women were still chattering. "I counted a good deal on those heifers," Canoc went on in the same open, confident, almost confiding way. "I have it in mind to build up a herd such as Blind Caddard had. So my hearty thanks to you, and the first calf one of them drops, bull or heifer as you please, is yours. You have only to send for it, Brantor Ogge."

There was just the one beat of silence, and then somebody near Canoc said, "Well said, well said!" and other voices joined in, but I did not hear Ogge speak.

The dinner was over at last, and my mother asked to be shown to her room, taking me with her. I heard Ogge then: "Oh, you'll not take young Orrec off already? He's not such a child as that, is he? Sit up with the men, boy, and taste my spring brewing!" But Melle pleaded that I was tired from the long day's ride, and the brantor's wife Denno said in her hoarse, tired voice, "Let the boy be for tonight, Ogge," and so we escaped, though my father had to stay and drink with the men.

It was late, I think, when he came up to the bedroom; I had been asleep, but I roused up when he knocked over a stool and made some other clatter.

"You're drunk!" Melle whispered, and he said, louder than he meant to, "Horse-piss beer!" She laughed, and he snorted.

"Where's the cursed bed!" he said, thumping about the room. They settled down. I lay on the cot under the window and listened to their whispering.

"Canoc, weren't you taking an awful risk?"

"Coming here at all was the risk."

"But about the heifers—"

"What's to gain by silence?"

"But you challenged him."

"To lie about it in front of his own people, who all know how the heifers got here—or to take the out I offered him."

"Hush, hush," she murmured, for his voice had got louder again. "Well, I'm glad he took the out."

"If he did. That's yet to see. Where's the girl? Did you see her yet?"

"What girl?"

"The bride. The blushing bride."

"Canoc, be quiet!" She was half scolding, half laughing.

"Shut my mouth then, love, shut my mouth for me," he whispered, and she laughed, and I heard the creak of the bed boards. They talked no more, and I slipped back into the luxury of sleep.

◆　◆　◆

THE NEXT DAY Brantor Ogge sent for my mother to join him as he showed my father about his establishment, the buildings and barns and stables, and I had to come along. No other women were with us, only his sons and some of the men of Drummant. Ogge talked to my mother in a strange, artificial way, patronising yet with a wheedling note. He spoke of her to the other men as if she were a pretty animal, talking about her ankles, her hair, the way she walked. When he talked to her, he often mentioned her Lowland origin with half-joking contempt. He seemed to be trying to remind her or himself that she was inferior to him. Yet he stuck to her side like a great leech. I tried to be between her and him, but he always got next to her on the other side of her as we walked about. Several times he suggested, all but ordered her, to send me off with "the other children" or with my father. She never refused to do so, but answered lightly, with a smile in her voice, and somehow did not do so.

As we returned to the Stone House, Ogge told us that he was planning a boar hunt up in the hills north of Drummant. They had been waiting, he said, for Parn, Gry's mother, to come before they set off. He pressed us to come on the hunt. My mother demurred, and he said, "Well, women don't belong on a pig hunt after all. Dangerous business. But send the boy along, it'll give him a change from moping about in his blindfold, eh? And if the boar charges, he can flick an eye at him and goodbye pig, eh? Eh, lad? Always a good thing to have a quick eye along on a pig hunt."

"It'll have to be mine, then," my father said, in the unfailingly pleasant tone he had here at Drummant. "A bit too much risk, yet, with Orrec."

"Risk? Risk? Afraid of the pig, is he?"

"Oh, not the risk for him," said Canoc. The tip of his fencing sword just touched Ogge that time.

Ogge had dropped his pretense of not knowing why my eyes were sealed, since it was clear that everybody else at Drummant knew why, and indeed believed all the wilder versions of my exploits. I was the boy with the destroying eye, the gift so powerful I couldn't control it, the new Blind Caddard. Ogge struck out with his bludgeon, but his blows fell short; my reputation put us just out of his reach. But he had other weapons.

Among all the people we had met the night before and all the people round us this morning, we had not yet been introduced to the brantor's granddaughter, the daughter of his younger son Sebb Drum and Daredan Caspro. We had met the parents: Sebb had a jovial, booming voice like his father; Daredan had spoken to my mother and me kindly enough, in a weak voice that made me picture her as decrepit, though, as Canoc had said, she wasn't all that ancient, after all. When we went back into the house later in the morning, Daredan was there, but still the daughter had not been brought forth, the girl who was, perhaps, to be my betrothed. The bride, the blushing bride, Canoc had called her last night, and at the thought I blushed.

As if he had the Morga gift of knowing what was in your mind, Ogge said in his loud voice, "You'll have to wait a few days to meet my granddaughter Vardan, young Caspro. She's down at the old Rimm house with her cousins. What's the use of meeting a girl you can't see, I was going to say, but then of course there's other ways to get to know a girl, as you'll find out, eh? Even more enjoyable ways, eh?" The men round us laughed. "She'll be here when we're back from pigsticking."

Parn Barre arrived that afternoon, and then all the talk was of the hunt. I had to go along. My mother wanted to forbid me to go, but I knew there was no way out of it, and said, "Don't worry, Mother. I'll be on Roanie, and it'll be all right."

"I'll be with him," Canoc said. I knew my prompt stoicism had pleased him deeply.

We left before dawn the next morning. Canoc stayed right beside me, on horseback and afoot. His presence was my only rock in an endless confusion, a black meaningless wilderness of riding and stopping and shouting and coming and going. It went on and on. We were gone five days. I could never get my bearings; I never knew what lay before my face or feet. Never was the temptation stronger to lift my blindfold, and yet never had I feared so much to do so, for I was in a continuous, terrified rage—helpless, resentful, humiliated. I dreaded and could not escape Brantor Ogge's shouting, harrying voice. Sometimes he pretended to believe I was truly blind and pitied me loudly, but mostly he teased and dared me, never quite openly, to lift my blindfold and display my destroying power. He feared me, and resented his fear, and wanted to make me suffer for it; and he was curious, because my power was unknown. He never overstepped certain lines with Canoc, for he understood clearly what Canoc could do. But what could I do? Might my blindfold be a trick, a bluff? Ogge was like a child teasing a chained dog to see if it really would bite. I was in his chains and at his mercy. I hated him so much that I felt that if I saw him, nothing could stop me, I would, I must destroy him, like the rat, like the adder, like the hound....

Parn Barre called a herd of wild swine down out of the foothills of Mount Airn, and called the boar away from the sows. When the dogs and hunters had the beast encircled, she left the hunt and came back to the camp, where I had been left along with the packhorses and the servants.

It had been a shameful moment for me when they all set off. "You're bringing the boy along, aren't you, Caspro?" Brantor Ogge said, and my father replied as pleasantly as ever that neither I nor old Roanie were coming, for fear of holding others back. "So then you'll be staying safe with him too?" came the big braying voice, and Canoc's soft one: "No, I thought I'd come to the kill."

He touched my shoulder before he mounted—he had brought Greylag, not the colt—and whispered, "Hold fast, my son." So I held fast, sitting alone among Drum's serfs and servants, who kept clear of me and soon forgot I was there, talking and joking loudly with one another. I had no idea of what was around me except the roll of bedding I had slept in the night before, which lay near my left hand. The rest of the universe was unknown, a blank gulf in which I would be lost the instant I stood up and took a step or two. I found some little stones in the dirt under my hand and played with them, handling them, counting them, trying to pile them or put them in lines, to pass the dreary time. We scarcely know how much of our pleasure and interest in life comes to us through our eyes until we have to do without them; and part of that pleasure is that the eyes can choose where to look. But the ears can't choose where to listen. I wanted to hear the birds singing, for the forest was full of their spring music, but mostly I heard only the men yelling and guffawing, and could only think what a noisy race we humans are.

I heard a single horse coming into camp, and the men's voices became less boisterous. Presently someone spoke near me: "Orrec, I'm Parn," she said. I felt her kindness in saying who she was, though I knew her voice, which was much like Gry's. "I've got a bit of fruit here. Open your hand." And she put two or three dried plums in my hand. I thanked her and chewed away on them. She had sat down near me and I could hear her chewing too.

"Well," she said, "by now the boar's killed a dog or two, and one or two men, maybe, but probably not, and they've killed him. And they're gutting him and cutting poles to carry him, and the dogs are after the guts, and the horses want to get away from it all but they can't." She spat. Maybe a plum pit.

"Do you never stay for the kill?" I asked timidly.

Though I had known her all my life, Parn always daunted me.

"Not with boar and bear. They'd want me to interfere, hold the beast so they could kill it. Give them an unfair advantage."

"But with deer, or hares—?"

"They're prey. A quick kill's best. Boar and bear aren't prey. They deserve their fair fight."

It was a clear position, with its own justice; I accepted it.

"Gry's got a dog for you," Parn said.

"I was going to ask her..."

"As soon as she heard about your eyes being sealed, she said you'd want a guide dog. She's been working with one of our shepherd Kinny's pups. They're good dogs. Come by Roddmant on your way home. Gry might have her ready for you."

That was a good moment, the only good moment of those endless, wretched days.

The hunters came back late to camp, straggling in. I was anxious about my father, of course, but dared not ask and only listened for what other men said, and for his voice. He came at last, leading Greylag, who had hurt his leg a little in some kind of collision or melee.

He greeted me gently, but I could tell he was exasperated almost beyond endurance. The hunt had been
mismanaged, Ogge and his elder son quarreling about
tactics and confusing everyone, so that the boar, though
brought to bay, had killed two dogs and escaped, a
horse had broken its leg in the chase, then as the boar
had got into thickets, the hunt had to dismount and go
in afoot, and another dog had been disemboweled, and
finally, as Canoc put it, very low-voiced, to me and
Parn, "they all stuck and stabbed at the poor brute but
none of them dared get close to it. It took half an hour
to kill it."

We sat in silence, hearing Ogge and his son shouting at each other. The hunt servants finally brought the
boar into camp; I smelled the rank wild stench of it and
the metallic smell of blood. The liver was ceremonially
divided up to be toasted over the fire by those who had
been in at the kill. Canoc did not go to get his share. He
went to look after our horses. I heard Ogge's son Harba
shouting at him to come get his killfeast, but I did not
hear Ogge call to him, nor did Ogge come to harass me
as his custom was. That night, and all the time it took
us to return to the Stone House of Drummant, Ogge
did not say a word to Canoc or to me. It was a relief to

be spared his jovial bullying, but it worried me too. I asked my father, when we camped the last night, if the brantor was angry with him.

"He says I refused to save his dogs," Canoc said. We lay by the warm ashes of a fire, head to head, whispering. I knew it was dark, and could pretend that it was because it was dark that I couldn't see.

"What happened?"

"The boar was slashing the dogs open. He yelled to me, 'Use your eye, Caspro!' As if I'd use my gift on a hunt! I went at the boar with my spear, along with Harba and a couple of others. Ogge didn't come in with us. The boar broke then, and ran right past Ogge, and got away. Ach, it was a botch, a butchery. And he lays it on me."

"Do we have to stay, when we get back there?"

"A night or so, yes."

"He hates us," I said.

"Not your mother."

"Her most," I said.

Canoc did not understand me, or did not believe me. But I knew it was true. Ogge could bully me all he liked, he could prove his superiority to Canoc in wealth and strength and so on, but Melle Aulitta was out of his reach. I had seen how he looked at her when he came to our house. I knew he looked at her here with that same amazement and hate and greed. I knew how he pressed close to her; I had heard his impotent attempts to impress her, boasting and patronising, and her mild, smiling replies, to which he had no reply. Nothing he had, or did, or was, could touch her. She did not even really fear him.

When we got back from the days and nights in the wilderness, and I could rejoin my mother, and bathe, and put on a clean shirt, even the unfriendly rooms of Drummant, which I had never seen, seemed familiar.

We went down to dinner in the great hall, and there I heard Brantor Ogge speak to my father for the first time in two days. "Where's your wife, Caspro?" he was saying. "Where's the pretty calluc? And your blind boy? Here's my granddaughter come to meet him, come across the whole domain, clear from Rimmant. Here, boy, come meet Vardan, let's see what you make of each other!" There was a brassy, crowing laughter in his voice.

I heard Daredan Caspro, the girl's mother, murmur to her to come forward. My mother, her hand on my arm, said, "We're happy to meet you, Vardan. This is my son Orrec."

I did not hear the girl say anything, but I heard a kind of sniggering or whimpering noise, so that I wondered if she was carrying a puppy that was making that sound.

"How do you do," I said, with a bob of the head.

"Do you do you do you," someone said in front of me, a thick, weak voice, where the girl must be.

"Say how do you do, Vardan." That was Daredan's tremulous whisper.

"Do you do, do you do."

I was speechless. My mother said, "Very well, thank you, my dear. It's a long way from Rimmant, isn't it. You must be quite tired."

The whimpering, puppyish sound began again.

"Yes, she is," her mother began, but Ogge's big voice, right next to us, broke in, "Well, well, let the young people talk to each other, don't be putting words in their mouths, you women! No matchmaking! Though they're a fine pair, aren't they? What do you say, boy, is she pretty, my granddaughter? She's got the same blood as you, you know, not calluc blood, but

Caspro blood. True lineage will out, they always say! Is she pretty, eh?"

"I can't see her, sir. I imagine she is."

Mother squeezed my arm, I don't know whether in terror at my boldness or encouraging my effort to be civil.

"Can't see her! I can't see her sir!" Ogge mimicked. "Well, let her lead you about then. She can see. She has fine eyes. Fine, sharp, keen, Caspro eyes. Don't you, girl? Don't you?"

"Do you do. Don't you. Don't you. Mama, can I want to stairs."

"Yes, dear. We will. It was a long ride, she's quite tired, please forgive us, Father-in-Law, we'll have a little rest before dinner."

The girl and her mother escaped. We could not. We had to sit for hours at the long table. The boar had been roasting all day on the spit. There were shouts of triumph as the head was carried in. Toasts were drunk to the hunters. The strong reek of boar's flesh filled the hall. Slabs of it were piled on my plate. Wine was poured, not beer or ale, but red wine from the vineyards in the southwest of the domain; only Drummant in all the Uplands made wine. It was heavy and sweet-sour. Ogge was soon louder-voiced than ever, shouting down his elder son and making much of the younger, Vardan's father. "So, how about a betrothal party, Sebb?" he would bellow, and laugh, not waiting for any answer, and then again after half an hour, "So, how about a betrothal party? Hey, Sebb? All our friends here. All under our roof. Caspros, Barres, Cordes, and Drums. The best blood of all the Uplands. Hey, Brantor Canoc Caspro, what do you say? Will you come? Here's a toast. Here's to friendship, loyalty, love, and marriage!"

Mother and I were not allowed to go upstairs after dinner. We had to stay in the great hall while Ogge Drum and his people drank themselves drunk. He was always near us, and talked a great deal to my mother. His tone and words grew more and more offensive, but neither Melle nor Canoc, who kept as close to us as he could, could be provoked to answer angrily, or to answer much at all. And after a time the brantor's wife intervened, staying with us as a kind of shield to my mother, answering Ogge for her. He grew sullen then and went off to quarrel again with his elder son, and we at last were able to slip out of the room and upstairs.

"Canoc, can we leave—go? Now?" my mother said in a whisper, in the long stone passage that led to our room.

"Wait," he answered. We got to our room and shut the door. "I need to talk to Parn Barre. We'll go early. He won't do us any harm tonight."

She gave a kind of laugh of despair.

"I'll be with you," he said. She let go of my arm to hold him and be held.

That was all as it should be, and I was very glad to hear we were going to escape, but I had a question that needed an answer.

"The girl," I said. "Vardan."

I felt them look at me, and there was a little silence while no doubt their eyes met.

"She's small, and not ugly," my mother said, "She has a sweet smile. But she's…"

"An idiot," my father said.

"No, Canoc, not that bad— But…not right. She's like a child, I think, in her mind. A little child. I don't think she'll ever be anything more."

"An idiot," my father repeated. "This is what Drum offered us as a wife for you, Orrec."

"Canoc," my mother murmured, scared, as I was, by the fiery hatred in his voice.

There was a knocking at our door. My father went to answer it. There were low-voiced consultations. After some while he came back, without my mother, to where I was sitting on the edge of my cot. "The child's been taken with seizures," he said, "and Daredan's asked for your mother to help her. Melle made fast friends with most of the women here, while we were out pig hunting and making enemies." He gave a humorless, weary laugh. I could hear him sit down, letting himself down all at once like a tired hound, in the chair before the unlit hearth. "I wish we were out of here, Orrec!"

"So do I," I said.

"Lie down and sleep. I'll wait for your mother."

I wanted to wait for her too, and tried to sit up with him; but he came and pushed me over gently onto the cot and covered me with the fine, warm woollen blanket, and I was asleep the next moment.

I woke suddenly and was wide awake. A cock was crowing away down in the barnyards. It might be dawn, or long before dawn. There was some small noise in the room, and I said, "Father?"

"Orrec? Are you awake? It's dark, I can't see." My mother felt her way to my cot and sat down beside me. "Oh, I'm so cold!" she said. She was shivering violently. I tried to put the warm blanket up around her shoulders, and she pulled it around us both.

"Where's Father?"

"He said he had to talk to Parn Barre. He says we'll

leave as soon as there's light to see by. I told Denno and Daredan we were leaving. They understand. I just said we had been away too long and Canoc was worried about the spring plowing."

"What was wrong with the girl?"

"She gets overtired easily and has spasms, and her mother is frightened by it, poor thing. I sent her off to get some sleep, she doesn't get much, and sat with the little girl. And then I half fell asleep there, and I don't know…It seemed…I got so cold, I can't seem to get warm…" I hugged her, and she snuggled up next to me. "Finally some of the other women came and could stay with the child, and I came back here, and your father went to find Parn. I suppose I should get our things ready to go. But it's so dark still. I keep looking for the dawn."

"Stay and get warm," I said, and we sat there trying to warm each other until my father came back. He had his flint and steel and could light a candle, and my mother hurried our few things together into the saddle-bag. We stole through the halls and passages and down the stairs and out of the house. I could smell dawn in the air, and the cocks were crowing as if they meant it. We went to the stables, where a sleepy, surly fellow roused up and helped us saddle our horses. My mother led Roanie out and held her while I mounted. I sat in the saddle waiting.

I heard my mother make a little surprised, grieving noise. Hoofs clopped on the cobbles as another of the horses was led out. She said, "Canoc, look."

"Ach," he said in disgust.

"What is it?" I asked.

"The chicks," my father said, low-voiced. "His people set the basket down where your mother gave it to them. Left it. Left the birds to die."

He helped Melle mount Greylag, and then rode Branty out of the stable; the stable boy opened the courtyard gate for us, and we rode out.

"I wish we could gallop," I said. My mother in her anxiety thought I meant it and said, "We can't, dear," but Canoc, riding close behind me, gave a short laugh. "No," he said, "we'll run away at a walk."

The birds were all singing now from tree to tree, and I kept thinking, as my mother had, that I would soon see the light of dawn.

After we had ridden several miles, she said, "It was a stupid gift to bring to a house like that."

"Like that?" said my father. "So grand and great, you mean?"

"In their own eyes," said Melle Aulitta.

I said, "Father, will they say we ran away?"

"Yes."

"Then we shouldn't—should we?"

"If we stayed, Orrec, I'd kill him. And though I'd like to kill him in his own house, I can't pay the price of that pleasure. He knows it. But I will get a little of my own back."

I didn't know what he meant, nor did my mother, till in the middle of the morning we heard a horse coming up behind us. We were alarmed, but Canoc said, "It's Parn."

She drew up with us and greeted us in her husky voice that was like Gry's. "So, where are your cattle, Canoc?" she said.

"Under that hill, ahead there." And we jogged on. Then we stopped, and my mother and I dismounted. She led me to a grassy place by a stream where I could sit. She took Greylag and Roanie into the water to drink and cool their feet; but Canoc and Parn rode off, and soon I could not hear them at all. "Where are they going?" I asked.

"Into that meadow. He must have asked Parn to call the heifers."

And after what seemed a long time, during which

I listened nervously for the sound of pursuit and vengeance coming down the road and heard nothing but birdsong and the distant lowing of cattle, Mother said, "They're coming," and soon I heard the grass swishing at the legs of the animals, and Branty's greeting whuff to our horses, and my father's voice saying something with a laugh to Parn.

"Canoc," my mother said, and he replied at once, "It's all right, Melle. They're ours. Drum looked after them for us, and now I'm taking them home. It's all right."

"Very well," she said unhappily.

And soon we all went on together, she first, then I, then Parn with the two heifers following close behind her, and Canoc bringing up the rear. The cattle did not slow us down; young and lively, and of a hauling, plowing breed, they stepped right out with the horses and kept up a good pace all day. We came onto our own domain by mid-afternoon, and cut across the northern part of it, heading for Roddmant. It had been Parn's suggestion that we take the heifers there and leave them in the Rodd pastures for a while with their old herd. "A little less provocative," she said, "and a good deal harder for Drum to steal back."

"Unless he comes calling on you," Canoc said.

"That's as may be. I'll have no more to do with Ogge Drum in any way, except that if he wants a feud he'll have one."

"If he has it with you he has it with us," Canoc said, joyfully fierce.

I heard my mother whisper, "Ennu, hear and be here." That was always her prayer when she was worried or frightened. I had asked and she had told me long ago about Ennu, who smoothed the road, blessed the work, and mended quarrels. The cat was Ennu's creature, and the opal Melle always wore was her stone.

About the time I ceased to feel the western sun on my back, we came to the Stone House of Roddmant. I had heard barking for a mile before we got there. A sea of dogs came round our horses as we rode in, all welcoming us joyously. And Ternoc came out shouting welcome to us too, and in a moment somebody came and took hold of my leg as I sat on Roanie. It was Gry, pressing her face against my leg.

"Here then, Gry, let him get off his horse," Parn said in her dry voice. "Give him a hand."

"I don't need it," I said. I dismounted creditably, and found Gry holding my arm now instead of my leg, and pressing her face against it, and crying. "Oh, Orrec," she said. "Oh, Orrec!"

"It's all right, Gry, it's all right, really. It isn't—I'm not—"

"I know," she said, letting me go, and snuffling several times. "Hello, Mother. Hello, Brantor Canoc. Hello," and I could hear her and Melle having a hug and kiss. Then she was back beside me.

"Parn says you have a dog," I said, awkwardly enough, for the guilt of poor Hamneda's death weighed on me—not only his death, but even the choice of him, the choice that Gry had known to be wrong.

"Do you want to see her?"

"Yes."

"Come on."

She took me somewhere—even this house and grounds, that I knew almost as well as my own house, were a labyrinth and a mystery in my blindness—and said, "Wait," and after a minute or two said, "Coaly, sit. This is Coaly, Orrec. This is Orrec, Coaly."

I squatted down. Reaching out a little, I felt warm breath on my hand, and then the delicate touch of whiskers, and a polite wet tongue washing my hand. I felt forward cautiously, afraid of poking the dog's eye or making some wrong movement, but she sat still and I felt the silky, tightly curled hair of her head and neck, her high-held, soft, flopover ears. "She's a black herder?" I said in a whisper.

"Yes. Kinny's bitch had three pups last spring. This was the best one. The children made her a pet, and he'd started her as a sheepdog. I asked for her when I heard about your eyes. Here's her lead." Gry put a short, stiff leather leash in my hand. "Walk with her," she said.

I stood up, and felt the dog stand. I took one step, and found the dog right in front of my legs, immovable. I laughed, though I was embarrassed. "We won't get far this way!"

"It's because if you went that way you'd fall over the lumber Fanno left there. Let her show you."

"What do I do?"

"Say, 'Walk on' and her name."

"Walk on, Coaly," I said to the darkness at the end of the leather strap in my hand.

The strap tugged me gently to the right, then forward. I walked as boldly as I could, until the strap pulled me gently to stop.

"Back to Gry, Coaly," I said, turning.

The strap turned me a little farther round and then walked me back and stopped me.

"I'm here," said Gry right in front of me. Her voice was hoarse and abrupt.

I knelt, felt for the dog sitting on her haunches, and put my arm around her. A silky ear was against my face, the whiskers tickled my nose. "Coaly, Coaly," I said.

"I didn't use the calling with her, only at the very beginning, a couple of times," Gry said. From the location of her voice she was squatting down near me. "She learned as fast as if I had. She's bright. And steady. But you both need to work together."

"Should I leave her here then, and come back?"

"I don't think so. I can tell you some things not to do. And try not to ask too many things of her at once for a while. But I can come over and work with her with you. I'd like to do that."

"That would be good," I said. After the threats and passions and cruelties of Drummant, Gry's clear love and kindness, and the calm, trusting, trustworthy response of the dog, were too much for me. I hid my face in the curly, silky fur. "Good dog," I said.

✦ 12 ✦

When Gry and I went indoors at last, I was frightened to learn that my mother, dismounting, had fainted in my father's arms. They had taken her upstairs and put her to bed. Gry and I hung around feeling childish, useless, the way young people do when an adult is taken sick. Canoc came down at last. He came straight to me and said, "She'll be all right."

"Is she just tired?"

He hesitated, and Gry asked, "She didn't lose the baby?"

It was part of Gry's gift to know when there were two lives in one body. It was not part of ours. I am sure

Canoc had not known Melle was with child before this day; she may not have known it herself.

To me the news carried little meaning. A boy of thirteen is at a great remove from that portion of life; pregnancy and childbirth are abstract matters, nothing to do with him at all.

"No," Canoc said. He hesitated again and said, "She needs to rest."

His tired, toneless voice troubled me. I wanted him to cheer up. I was sick of fear and gloom. We were out of all that, free again, with our friends, safe at Rodd-mant. "If she's all right for a while, maybe you could come see Coaly," I said.

"Later," he said. He touched my shoulder and went off. Gry took me round to the kitchen, for in the commotion nothing had been done about supper, and I was ravenous. The cook stuffed us with rabbit pie. Gry said I was a disgusting sight with gravy all over my face, and I said let her try eating what she couldn't see, and she said she had tried it—she had blindfolded herself for a full day, to find what it was like for me. When we had eaten we went back outdoors, and Coaly took me for a walk in the dark. There was a half moon that gave Gry some light to see her way by, but she said Coaly and I were getting on better than she was, and fell over a root to prove it.

When we were children together at Roddmant, Gry and I used to sleep wherever we fell asleep, like any young animals; but since then there had been talk of betrothals and such matters. We said goodnight like adults. Ternoc took me to my parents' room. Roddmant had no such array of bedrooms and beds as Drummant. Ternoc whispered to me that my mother was asleep in the bed, my father in the chair; he gave me a blanket, and I rolled myself up on the floor and slept there.

In the morning my mother insisted she was quite well. She had taken a little chill, nothing more. She was ready to go home. "Not on horseback," Canoc said, and Parn seconded him. Ternoc offered us a hay cart and the daughter of the droop-lipped mare that had borne him into battle at Dunet. So Mother and Coaly and I traveled to Caspromant in luxury, on rugs spread on straw in the cart, while Canoc rode Branty, and Greylag and Roanie followed willingly behind, all of us glad to be going home.

Coaly seemed to accept her change of house and owner with a tranquil heart, though she had to do an immense amount of sniffing around the house, and pissed her mark on various bushes and stones outside it. She politely greeted the few old hounds we had, but kept aloof from them. Her sheep-herding breed wasn't sociable and democratic as they were, but reserved and intent. She was like my father: she took her responsibilities seriously. I was her chief responsibility.

Gry soon rode over to continue our training, and came every few days. She rode a colt called Blaze, who belonged to the Barres of Cordemant. They had asked Parn to break him, and Parn was training both the colt and her daughter in horsebreaking. Callers use that word, though it has little to do with how they train a young horse. Nothing is broken in that education; rather something is made one, made whole. It's a long process. Gry explained it to me thus: we ask a horse to do things which the horse would by nature rather not do; and a horse doesn't submit its will to ours the way a dog does, being a herd animal not a pack animal, and preferring consensus to hierarchy. The dog accepts; the horse agrees. All this Gry and I discussed at length, while Coaly and I went about learning our duties to each other. And we talked about it when we went riding, Gry and Blaze learning and teaching their duties to each other, and I on Roanie, who had long since learned all she needed to know. Coaly came along with us, off her leash, on holiday, free to trot, stop, sniff, take side trails, and start rabbits without worrying about me. But if I said her name, she was there.

Coaly and Gry made such a difference to my life that I remember that summer, the first I spent in darkness, as a bright one. There had been so much trouble and stress before it, I had been in such perplexity and terror concerning my gift. Now, with my eyes sealed, I had no possibility of using it or misusing it, and need not torment myself or be tormented. Once the nightmare of Drummant was past, I was among my own people. And the awe I inspired in some of the simpler ones was a compensation, though I didn't admit it, for my helplessness. While you're groping and blundering your way across a room, it can hearten you to hear somebody whispering, "What if he lifted his blindfold! I'd die of fear!"

My mother was unwell for a while after we got home and kept to her bed. Then she got up and began to go about the house as before; but one night at supper I heard her rise and say something in a frightened voice, and there was a commotion, and she and my father both left the room. I sat at table bereft, confused. I had to ask the women of the house what had happened. At first no one would tell me, but then one of the girls said, "Oh, she's bleeding, her skirts were all bloody." I was terrified. I went to the hall and sat in the hearth seat alone in a kind of daze. My father found me there at last. All he could say was that it was a miscarriage, and she was doing well enough. He spoke calmly, and I was reassured. I grasped at reassurance.

Gry came over on Blaze the next day. We went up to see my mother in her small tower room. There was a cot-bed there, and the room was warmer than the bedroom. A fire burned on the hearth, though it was full summer. Melle had her warmest shawl round her shoulders, as I knew from her embrace. Her voice was a little weak and hoarse but she sounded entirely herself. "Where's Coaly?" she said. "I need a visit from Coaly." Coaly was of course there in the room, for she and I were inseparable now; and she was invited up onto the bed, where she lay tensely alert, apparently believing my mother needed a guard dog. Mother asked about our lessons at guiding and being guided, and about Gry's horsebreaking, and we chatted along just as usual. But Gry got up before I was ready to go. She said we must be going, and as she kissed my mother she whispered, "I'm sorry about the baby."

Melle murmured to her, "I have you two."

My father was gone from daybreak to evening every day at the work of the domain. I had begun to be of use to him, but was useless now. Alloc took my place at his side. Alloc was a clear-hearted man, without ambitions or pretensions; he thought of himself as stupid, and some people agreed with him, but though slow to think, he often grasped an idea without thinking about it, and his judgment was usually sound. He and Canoc worked together, and he was what I could not be. I was both jealous and envious of him. I had the self-respect not to show it; for it would have hurt Alloc, angered my father, and done me no good.

When my uselessness and helplessness carked me, when my own resolution weakened and I yearned to untie my blindfold and take back my whole lost inheritance of light, I came up against the immovable figure of my father. Seeing, I was a mortal danger to Canoc and to all his people. With my eyes sealed, I was his shield and support. My blindness was my use.

He had talked to me a little about the visit to Drummant, saying that he thought Ogge Drum had feared us both, but me most, and that his cruel teasing and scoffing had been a bluff, a show, to save face among his people. "What he most wanted was to drive us away. He was longing to test you, all right, but every time he was about to force you to act, he drew back. He didn't dare. And he didn't challenge me, for fear of you."

"But that girl—he was using her to humiliate us!"

"He'd set that up before we knew of your wild gift. Caught himself in his own trap. He had to go through with it, to show he didn't fear us. But he does, Orrec. He does."

Our two white heifers were back at Caspromant, in with the herd in the high pastures, a long way from the borders of Drummant. Drum had said nothing about them and had made no retaliatory move on us or Roddmant. "I gave him his out, and he took it," Canoc said with the vindictive glee that seemed to be his only cheer these days. He was always tense, always grim. With me and with my mother he was tender and cautious, but he never was with us for long, out at his work, or coming in silent with weariness, heavy with sleep.

Melle grew stronger slowly. There was a meek, patient note in her voice when she was unwell that I hated to hear. I wanted to hear her clear laugh, her quick step through the rooms. She went about the house now, but tired easily, and whenever there was a rainy day or the wind coming down from the Carrantages chilled the summer evening, she had a fire in the tower room and sat huddled by it in the heavy shawl of undyed brown wool that my father's mother had woven for her. Once, sitting there with her, I said without thinking about it, "You've been cold ever since Drummant."

"Yes," she said. "I have. That last night. When I went to sit with the little girl. That was so strange. I don't think I ever told you about it, did I? Denno had gone downstairs to try to stop her sons from quarreling. Poor Daredan was so worn out, I told her to go sleep a while, I'd stay with Vardan. The poor little thing was asleep, but she always seemed to be just about to wake up, with the twitches and spasms that ran through her. So I put out the light and was drowsing along beside her, and after a while I thought I heard somebody whispering or chanting. A kind of droning. I thought I was in our house in Derris and Father was leading a service downstairs. I must have been nearly asleep myself. And it went on and on and then it died away. And I realised that I wasn't back home but at Drummant, and the fire had burned nearly out, and I was so cold I could hardly move. Cold to the bone. And the little girl was lying still as death. That scared me, and I got up to look at her, but she was breathing. And then Denno came in, and gave me a candle to come back to our room with. And Canoc wanted to go find Parn, so he left, and the door closing blew out the candle. And the fire was out. You woke, so I sat there in the dark with you, and I couldn't get warm. You remember that. And the whole ride home, my feet and hands were like lumps of ice. Ah! I wish we'd never gone there, Orrec!"

"I hate them."

"The women were kind to me."

"Father says Ogge was afraid of us."

"I return the compliment," Melle said with a little shudder.

When I told this tale to Gry—for I told Gry everything but the things I kept secret from myself—I could ask her what I hadn't wanted to ask my mother: Could Ogge Drum have come into that room while she was there? "Father says the Drums work their power with words, spells, as well as eye and hand. Maybe what she heard…"

Gry did not like that idea at all, and resisted it. "But why would he use it on her, not on you or Canoc? Melle couldn't do him any harm!"

I thought of Canoc saying, "Wear your red gown, so

he can see the gift he gave me." That was the harm. But I hardly knew how to say it. All I could say was, "He hated us all."

"Did she tell your father about that night?"

"I don't know. I don't know if she thinks it's important. You know, she doesn't…she doesn't think about the gifts, the powers, very much. I don't know even what she thinks about me, now. About the wild gift. She knows why we sealed my eyes. But I don't think she believes…" I stopped, unsure of what I was saying and feeling myself on dangerous ground. Automatically I put my hand out to Coaly's warm curly back as she lay stretched out beside my leg. But even Coaly couldn't guide me in this darkness.

"Maybe you should tell Canoc," Gry said.

"It would be better if Mother did."

"You told me."

"But you're not Canoc," I said, an obvious fact which contained a great deal of unsaid meaning. Gry understood it.

"I'll ask Parn if there's anything people can do… about that power," she said.

"No, don't." Telling Gry was all right, but if the story went further I would have betrayed my mother's confidence.

"I won't say why I'm asking."

"Parn will know why."

"Maybe she already does... When you came to our place, that night. When Melle fainted. Mother said to Father, 'He may have touched her.' I didn't know what she meant, then. I thought maybe she meant Ogge had tried to rape Melle, and hurt her."

We sat brooding. The idea that Ogge had cast a wasting spell on my mother was hideous yet vague, hard to contemplate. My mind slid away from it, drifting to other things.

"She hasn't said anything about Annren Barre since she was at Drummant," Gry remarked, meaning her mother not mine.

"They're still quarreling at Cordemant. Raddo said it's an open feud between the brothers. They're living at opposite ends of the domain, they won't get within eyesight of each other for fear of going blind or deaf."

"Father says neither of the brothers has the full gift, but their sister Nanno does. Nanno says if they go on quarreling she'll make them both into mutes, so they can't speak the curse." She laughed, and so did I. Such grotesque cruelties were funny to us. And I was suddenly light-hearted, too, because Parn was no longer talking of betrothing Gry to the boy at Cordemant.

"Mother says wild gifts are sometimes just very strong gifts. And it takes years to learn to use them." Gry's voice was husky, as it always was when she said something important.

I made no answer. None was needed. If Parn had meant that she believed my gift to be strong and to be ultimately controllable, she was saying that I might, in time, be a fit match for Gry. That was enough for us.

"I want to try the Ashbrook path," I said, jumping up. Sitting and talking was all very well, but getting outside and riding was much better. I was full of hope and energy now, because Parn Barre who was wise had said I would be able to use my eyes again, and marry Gry, and kill Ogge Drum with a glance if he ever dared come near Caspromant....

We rode along the Ashbrook. I asked Gry to tell me when we came to the destroyed hillside. We reined in the horses there. Coaly went running on ahead. When Gry called her back she came, but with a whimper, which was eloquent, since she very seldom said anything at all. "Coaly doesn't like it here," Gry said.

I asked her to describe the place. The grass was growing back, she said, but it still had a strange look. "All crumbled. Just lumps and dust. Nothing has any shape."

"Chaos."

"What's Chaos?"

"It's in Mother's story about the beginning of the world. At first there was stuff floating around, but none of it had any shape or form. It was all just bits and crumbs and blobs, not even rocks or dirt, just stuff. With no forms or colors, and no ground or sky, or up and down, or north and south. No sense to anything. No direction. Nothing connected or related. It wasn't dark, it wasn't light. A mess. Chaos."

"Then what happened?"

"Nothing ever would have happened if bits of stuff hadn't stuck together a little, here and there. So the stuff began to make shapes. First just clods and lumps of dirt. Then stones. And the stones rubbed together and made sparks of fire, or melted one another till they ran as water. The fire and the water met and made steam, fog, mist, air—air the Spirit could breathe. Then the Spirit gathered itself together and drew breath, and spoke. It said everything that was to be. It sang to the earth and fire and water and air, singing all the creatures into being. All the shapes of mountains and rivers, the shapes of trees, and animals, and men. Only it took no shape itself, and gave itself no name, so that it could remain everywhere, in all things and between all things, in every relation and every direction. When everything is unmade at the end and Chaos returns, the Spirit will be in it as it was in the beginning."

After a while Gry asked, "But it won't be able to breathe?"

"Not until it all happens over again."

Enlarging it, going into detail, and supplying an answer to Gry's question, I had gone somewhat beyond the bounds of my mother's story. I often did so. I had no sense of the sacredness of a story, or rather they were all sacred to me, the wonderful word-beings which, so long as I was hearing or telling them, made a world I could enter seeing, free to act: a world I knew and understood, that had its own rules, yet was under my control as the world beyond the stories was not. In the boredom and inactivity of my blindness, I lived increasingly in these stories, remembering them, asking my mother to tell them, and going on with them myself, giving them form, speaking them into being as the Spirit did in Chaos.

"Your gift is very strong," Gry said in her husky voice.

I remembered then where we were. And I was ashamed of bringing Gry here, as if I'd wanted her to see what my power had done. Why had I wanted to bring her here?

"That tree," I said, "there was a tree—" And I blurted out, "I thought it was my father. I thought I'd— I didn't even know what I was looking at—"

I could say no more. I signaled Roanie to go on, and we left the ruined place. After a while Gry said, "It's starting to grow back, Orrec. The weeds and the grass. I guess the Spirit is still in it."

◆ 13 ◆

Autumn went along much as summer had, with no great events to mark it. We heard that ever since our visit the quarrel between Brantor Ogge and his elder son Harba, that began on the boar hunt, had grown into enmity. Harba had taken his wife and people down to Rimmant and was living there, while the younger son, Sebb, was ensconced in the Stone House of Drummant, treated as the heir and brantor-to-be. But Sebb and Daredan's daughter Vardan had been ill all summer and was wasting away, going from seizure to convulsion to paralysis, and such mind as she had ever had was gone. We heard all about this from a travelling blacksmith's wife. Such people are great and useful gossips, carrying news from one domain to the other all over the Uplands, and we listened eagerly, though the woman's callous relish of details of the child's illness disgusted me. I didn't want to hear all that. I felt that I was in some way responsible for the girl's misery.

When I asked myself how that could possibly be, I saw in my mind's eye the face of Ogge Drum, pouched and creased, with drooping eyelids and an adder's gaze.

Gry couldn't come to visit me often while the work of harvest was going on and every hand was needed every day. And there was no need for her to give Coaly and me further training; we were by now, as my mother said, a six-legged boy with an unusually keen sense of smell.

But along in October, Gry rode Blaze over for the day, and after Coaly and I had shown her whatever our new achievements were, we settled down, as always, to talk. We discussed the quarrels at Cordemant and Drummant, and remarked sagely that as long as they were busy feuding with their own people they were less apt to invade and poach and thieve across their borders. We mentioned Vardan. Gry had heard that the child was dying.

"Could it have been Ogge, do you think?" I asked. "That night. When my mother was there, and heard… He could have been casting his power on the girl."

"And not on Melle?"

"Maybe not." I had worked out this hopeful idea some while ago and it had seemed plausible to me; spoken, less so.

"Why would he put the wasting on his own granddaughter?"

"Because he was ashamed of her. Wanted her dead. She was…" I heard the thick, weak voice, *Do you do, do you do.* "She was an idiot," I said harshly. And I thought of the dog Hamneda.

Gry did not say anything. I had the sense that she wanted to speak but found she couldn't.

"Mother's been much better," I said. "She walked all the way to the Little Glen with Coaly and me."

"That's good," Gry said. She did not say and I would not think that, six months ago, such a walk would have been nothing to Melle; she would have gone on with me and climbed to the spring in the high hills and come home singing. I would not think the thought but it was there. I said, "Tell me what she looks like."

That was an order Gry never disobeyed; when I asked her to be my eyes, she tried as best she could to see for me. "She's thin," she said.

I knew that from her hands.

"She looks a little sad. But just as beautiful."

"She doesn't look ill?"

"No. Only thin. And tired, or sad. Losing the baby…"

I nodded. After a while I said, "She's been telling me a long story. It's part of Hamneda's story. About his friend Omnan, who went mad and tried to kill him. I can tell you part of it."

"Yes!" said Gry in a contented tone, and I could hear her settle herself to listen. I reached out to Coaly's back and left my hand there. That touch was my anchor in the unseen real world, while I launched out into the bright, vivid world of story.

Nothing we had said about my mother had been dire, or even discouraging, yet without saying it we had said that she was not well, that she was not getting better, that she was getting worse. We both knew it.

My mother knew it. She was bewildered and patient. She tried to be well. She couldn't believe that she couldn't do what she had used to do, or half what she had used to do. "This is so foolish," she would say, the nearest she ever came to complaint.

My father knew it. As the days shortened and the work lessened and he was home longer and more often, he had to see that Melle was weak, that she tired easily, that she ate little and had grown thin, that some days all she could do was sit by her fire in her brown shawl and shiver and doze. "I'll be well when it gets warm again," she would say. He would build up her fire and seek what else he could do, anything to do for her. "What can I bring you, Melle?" I could not see his face, but I heard his voice, and the tenderness of it made me wince with pain.

My blindfold and my mother's illness worked together in one way that was good: we both had time to indulge our love of storytelling, and the stories carried us out of the dark and the cold and the dreary boredom of being useless. Melle had a wonderful memory, and whenever she searched it she found in it another story she had been told or had read. If she forgot part of the tale, she, like me, filled in and invented freely, even if it was a story from the holy texts and rituals, for who was to be shocked and cry heresy, here? I told her she was a well: she let down the bucket and it came up full of stories. She laughed at that. And she said, "I'd like to write down some of the things in the bucket."

I couldn't prepare the linen and ink for her myself, but I could tell Rab and Sosso, our two young house-keepers, how to go about it, and they were happy to do anything for Melle.

These two women were Caspros through their fathers, neither of whom had had any gift of the lineage. They inherited their position in the household from their mothers, who, together with my mother, had trained them thoroughly. During Melle's illness they took full control of domestic matters, running the house according to her standards, and always plotting how to make her life easier. They were warmhearted, energetic women. Rab was engaged to be married to Alloc, though neither seemed to be in a hurry to marry. Sosso had announced that in her opinion there were enough men underfoot already.

They learned to stretch the canvas and mix the ink, and my father devised a kind of bed table, and Melle set to writing down all she could remember of the sacred tales and songs she had learned as a girl. Some days she wrote for two or three hours. She never said why she was writing. She never said that it was for me. She never said that to write was to affirm that one day I'd be able to read what she wrote. She never said that she wrote because she knew she might not be here to speak. She said only, when Canoc anxiously scolded her for wearing herself out at the writing, "It makes me feel that everything I learned when I was a girl isn't just going to waste. When I write it down, I can think about it."

So she would write in the morning, and rest in the afternoon. Towards evening Coaly and I would come to her room, and often Canoc, and she'd go on with whatever hero tale we were in the midst of, or a story of the time when Cumbelo was King, and we'd listen to her, there by the hearth, in the tower room, in the heart of winter.

Sometimes she said, "Orrec, you go on with it now." She wanted to know, she said, if I remembered the stories, if I could tell them well.

More and more often she began the story, and I ended it. One day she said, "I'm too lazy to tell a story. Tell me one."

"Which one?"

"Make one up."

How did she know I made stories up, following them in my mind through the long dull hours?

"I thought about some things Hamneda might have done while he was in Algalanda, that weren't in the story."

"Tell them."

"Well, after Omnan left him in the desert, you know, and he had to find his way alone...I thought about how thirsty he was. It was all dust, the desert, as far as the eye could see, hills and valleys of red dust. Nothing growing, no sign of a spring. If he didn't find water, he'd die there. So he began walking, going north by the sun, for no reason except that north was the way home to Bendraman. He walked and he walked, and the sun beat on his head and back, and the wind blew the dust in his eyes and nostrils so it was hard to breathe. The wind got stronger and began to blow the dust in circles, and a whirlwind rose up in front of him and came towards him, picking up the red dust and whirling it high. He didn't try to run away, but stood still and held out his arms, and the whirlwind came on him and picked him up, whirled him up into the air, coughing and choking with the dust. It carried him over the desert, whirling him round all the time and choking him. Finally the sun began to set. Then the wind dropped. And the whirlwind died down, and sank down, and dropped Hamneda at the gates of a city. His head was still whirling, he was too dizzy to stand up, and covered all over with red dust. He crouched there with his head down, trying to catch his breath, and the guards at the gate peered at him. It was twilight. One said, 'Somebody left a big clay jar there,' and the other one said, 'It's not a jar, it's a figure, a statue. A statue of a dog. It must be a gift to the king.' And they decided to carry it into the city…"

"Go on," Melle murmured. And I went on.

But now I come to a place in this story I do not want to go through. A desert. No whirlwind to pick me up and carry me across it.

Every day was one step farther into it.

There came a day when my mother put away the canvas and ink and said she was too tired to write any more for a while. There came a day when she asked me to tell a story, but shivered and dozed through it, not hearing it, only hearing my voice. "Don't stop," she said, when, thinking I was only making her more wretched, I tried to let my voice die away so she could sleep. "Don't stop."

At the edge of the desert you think it may be wide. You think it could take a month, maybe, to cross it. And two months go by, and three, and four, every day a step farther into the dust.

Rab and Sosso were kind and strong, but when Melle grew too weak to look after herself at all, Canoc told them that he would see to her needs. He did so with the most delicate patience, caring for her, lifting her, cleaning her, soothing her, trying to keep her warm. For two months he scarcely left the tower room. Coaly and I were there most of the day, if only to keep him silent company. At night he kept vigil alone.

He fell asleep sometimes in the daytime, beside her on the narrow bed; weak as she was, she would whisper, "Lie down, love. You must be tired. Keep me warm. Come under the shawl with me." And he would lie beside her, holding her close to him, and I would listen to their breathing.

May came. One morning I sat in the window seat, feeling the sunlight on my hands; I smelled the fragrances of spring, and heard the sound of the light wind moving in young leaves. Canoc lifted Melle so Sosso could change the sheet. She weighed so little now, he could pick her up in his arms like a little child. She cried out sharply. I did not know then what had happened. Her bones had grown so fragile that when he lifted her, they broke; her collarbone and thighbone snapped like sticks.

He set her down on the bed. She had fainted. Sosso hurried out to fetch help. It was the only time in all those months that Canoc gave way. He crouched down at the bedside and wept, loudly, gasping with a terrible sound, hiding his face in the sheets. I huddled in the window seat, hearing him.

They came with some idea of tying splints to her limbs to keep them in place, but he would not let them touch her.

The next day I was out at the gate of the courtyard, letting Coaly have a run, when Rab called me. Coaly came as quickly as I did. We went up to the tower room. Mother was lying among pillows, her old brown shawl about her shoulders; I felt it under my hand when I went to kiss her. Her hand and cheek were icy cold, but she returned my kiss. "Orrec," she whispered. "I want to see your eyes." And when she felt me resist, "You can't hurt me now, love," she whispered.

I still hesitated.

"Go on," Canoc said, across the bed from me, his voice quiet, as it always was in this room.

So I tugged the blindfold down and pulled the two pads away from my eyes, and tried to open my eyes. At first I thought I could not. I had to push up the lids with my fingers, and when I did, I saw nothing but a flashing, lancing, painful dazzle, a jumble, a chaos of light.

Then my eyes remembered their skill, and I saw my mother's face.

"There, there," she said, "that's right." Her eyes looked up into mine out of the little sunken ruin of her face and body, the tangle of black hair. "That's right," she said again quite strongly. "You keep this for me." She opened her hand. Her opal and the silver chain lay in it. She could not lift her hand to give it to me. I took it and put the chain over my head. "Ennu, hear and be here," she murmured. Then she closed her eyes.

I looked up at my father. His face was hard and set. He nodded very slightly.

I kissed my mother's cheek again, and put the pads over my eyes, and pulled up my blindfold.

Coaly tugged slightly at the leash, and I let her lead me out of the room.

That day a little after sunset my mother died.

· · ·

GRIEVING, LIKE BEING blind, is a strange business; you have to learn how to do it. We seek company in mourning, but after the early bursts of tears, after the

praises have been spoken, and the good days remembered, and the lament cried, and the grave closed, there
is no company in grief. It is a burden borne alone. How
you bear it is up to you. Or so it seems to me. Maybe in
saying so I'm ungrateful to Gry, and to the people of the
house and domain, my companions, without whom I
might not have carried my burden through the dark
year.

So I call it in my mind: the dark year.

To try to tell it is like trying to tell the passage of a
sleepless night. Nothing happens. One thinks, and
dreams briefly, and wakes again; fears loom and pass,
and ideas won't come clear, and meaningless words
haunt the mind, and the shudder of nightmare brushes
by, and time seems not to move, and it's dark, and nothing happens.

Canoc and I were not companions in our grief. We
could not be. However untimely and cruel my loss, I
had lost only what time must take and can replace. For
him there was no replacement; the sweetness of his life
was gone.

Because he was left solitary, and because he blamed
himself, his sorrow was hard, and angry, and found no
relief.

After Melle's death some of the people of the domain went in fear of Canoc as well as me. I had the wild gift, and now what might not he do in his bitter grief? We were the descendants of Caddard. And we had legitimate cause for anger. Every soul in Caspromant believed as a certainty that Ogge Drum had killed Melle Aulitta. She died a year and a day after the night we left Drummant. There was no need of the story she had told me and I had told Gry of that last night there, the whispering and the cold. We had told it to no one; I never knew whether she told it to Canoc. All he or anyone needed to know was that she had gone to Drummant a beautiful and radiant woman, and had come back ill, to lose the child she carried, and waste away, and die.

Canoc was a strong man, but the last months had taken a hard toll on both his body and mind. He was worn out. For the first halfmonth he slept a great deal—in her room, in the bed where he had held her as she died. He spent hours alone there. Rab and Sosso and the others were afraid for him and afraid of him. They used me as go-between. "Just slip up there, will you, and make sure the brantor's not needing anything," the women would say, and Alloc or one of the other men would say, "Just go up and ask the brantor does he want the horse to have bran or oats?"—for old Greylag was off his feed, and they were concerned about him. Coaly and I would go up the curving stone stairs to the tower room, and I would get up my nerve and knock. Sometimes he answered, sometimes not. When he did open the door, his voice was cold and flat. "Tell them no," he would say, or, "Tell Alloc to use his wits," and he would close the door again.

I dreaded to come where I was not wanted, but I had no physical fear of him. I knew he would never use his power against me, as Melle had known I would never use mine against her.

When I realised that, when I thought of it that way, a shock ran through me. This was no mere belief, it was knowledge. I knew he would not hurt me. I knew I would not have hurt her. So I could have taken off my blindfold, when I was with her. I could have seen her, all that last year. I could have cared for her, been useful to her, read to her, as well as telling my foolish stories. I could have seen her dear face not that once, but all year, all year long!

That idea brought me not tears, but a surge of anger that must have been something like what my father was feeling—a dry fury of impotent regret.

There was no one to punish for it but myself, or him.

On the night she died I had clung to him, and he had held me against him, my head on his chest. Since then he had scarcely touched me, and spoken very little to me; he had shut himself up in her room and held aloof. He wants his grief all to himself, I thought with a bitter heart.

◆ 14 ◆

All spring, Ternoc and Parn had come back and forth from Roddmant as often as they could. Ternoc was a kindly man, a follower not a leader, who was not very happy with his wilful wife but never complained of her. He had looked up to my father all his life; he had loved my mother dearly and mourned her now. Late in June he came over, went up to the tower room, and talked with Canoc for a long time. Canoc came downstairs to supper with him that evening, and from that day on ceased to lock himself away, returning to his work and duties, though he slept always in the tower room. He spoke to me, stiffly and with effort, as in duty bound. I responded the same way.

I had hoped Parn might know how to help my mother in her illness, but Parn was a hunter not a healer. She was uneasy in a sickroom, impatient, not of much use. At my mother's funeral, Parn had led the lament, the sobbing howl that Upland women raise over the grave. It is a hideous shrill clamor, going on and on and on, unbearable, the noise of animals in pain. Coaly raised her head and howled with the women, shuddering all over, and I too stood shuddering and fighting my tears. When it was over at last I was spent, exhausted, relieved. Canoc had stood through the lament unmoving, enduring it, like a rock in the rain.

Soon after Melle's death, Parn went up to the Carrantages. The people of Borremant had heard of her skill in calling to the hunt and sent for her to come. She wanted Gry to come with her, to begin to practice her gift. It was a rare chance to go among the wealthy highlanders and gain renown there. Gry refused. Parn got angry with her. Once again mild Ternoc intervened: "You go and come as you please," he said to his wife, "so let your daughter do the same." Parn saw the justice in that, though it didn't suit her. She went off the next day, without Gry, not bidding anyone goodbye.

The colt Blaze had been returned, fully trained, to Cordemant. When Gry came to us, she rode a plow horse, if one was free; if not she walked, a long walk to go and return in a day. It was too far for me to go alone on Roanie or to walk with Coaly. And Roanie was getting old, and though Greylag got over his distemper he too was an old horse now. Branty was a splendid four-year-old, much in demand as a stud, which suited him very well indeed, though it interfered with his other duties. Our stable was pretty thin. I said one night, gathering up my nerve as I always did when I spoke to my father now, "We should get a new colt."

"I'd thought of asking Danno Barre what he'd want for that grey mare."

"She's old. If we got a colt or a filly, Gry could train her."

When you cannot see the speaker, his silence is a mystery. I waited, not knowing if Canoc was considering what I said or had rejected it already.

"I'll look about," he said.

"Alloc says there's a lovely filly over at Callemmant. He heard about her from the smith."

This time the silence went on. I had to wait a month for the answer. It arrived in the shape of Alloc shouting at me to come out and see the new filly. I couldn't do that, but I could come and feel her coat, and

scratch her topknot, and swing up in the saddle for a
short led walk round the courtyard, Alloc praising her
manners and beauty all the way. She was just a year old,
he said, a bright bay, with a star, for which she was
named. "Can Gry come and work with her?" I asked,
and Alloc said, "Oh, she's to stay there at Roddmant for
a year or so and learn her job. She's too young a lass for
your father and me, see."

When Canoc came in that night, I wanted to thank
him. I wanted to go to him and put my arms around
him. But I was afraid of blundering in my blindness,
afraid of making a clumsy move, afraid he did not want
me to touch him.

I said, "I rode the filly, Father," and he said, "Good,"
and bade me goodnight, and I heard his weary tread on
the stairs up to the tower room.

◆ ◆ ◆

SO THROUGH the dark time, Gry could come to me
riding Star, two or three or four times in a halfmonth,
sometimes even oftener.

When she came we would go out riding together
and she would tell me what she and Star were doing.
The filly was as sweet as new bread, and as a riding

horse needed little teaching, so she was learning fancy
gaits and tricks, to show off the trainer, Gry said, as
well as the horse. We seldom rode far, for Roanie was
getting rheumatic. Then we'd come back to the Stone
House, and if it was warm we'd sit out in the kitchen
gardens, or in cold or rainy weather in the corner of the
great hearth, to talk.

There were many times in the first year after my
mother died that though I was glad Gry was there, I
could not talk. I had nothing to say. There was a blankness, a deadness around me I could not get through
with words.

Gry would talk a little, telling me what news she
had, and then fall into silence with me. It was as easy to
sit in silence with her as it was with Coaly. I was grateful to her for that.

I cannot remember much of that year. I had sunk
into the black blankness. There was nothing for me to
do. My only use was to be useless. I would never learn
to use my gift: only not to use it. I would sit here in the
hall of the Stone House and people would be afraid of
me, and that was all my purpose in life. I might as well
be an idiot like the poor child at Drummant. It would
make no difference. I was a bogey in a blindfold.

For days at a time I said nothing to anyone. Sosso and Rab and the other people about the house tried to talk to me, cheer me; they brought me tidbits from the kitchen; Rab was brave enough to offer me tasks to do in the household, things I needed no eyes to do and had done for her gladly when I was first blinded. Not now. Alloc would come in with my father at day's end, and they would talk a little, and I would sit with them in silence. Alloc would try to draw me into the conversation. I would not be drawn. Canoc would say to me, stiffly, "Are you well, Orrec?" or, "Did you ride today?" And I would say yes.

I think now he suffered as much as I did from our estrangement. All I knew then was that he was not paying the price I paid for our gift.

All through that winter, I made plans of how I could get to Drummant, get within sight of Ogge, and destroy him. I would have to take off the blindfold, of course. Over and over I imagined it: I would go out before daylight, taking Branty, for the older horses were not fast or strong enough. I'd ride all day to Drummant, and wait hidden somewhere till night, and wait till Ogge came out. No, better, I might disguise myself. The people at Drummant had only seen me with the blindfold, and I was growing taller, my voice had begun to deepen. I'd wear a serf's cloak, not the coat and kilt. They wouldn't know me. I'd leave Branty hidden in the woods, for he was a horse people would recognise, and I'd stroll in on foot, like a roving farmer lad from the Glens, and wait till Ogge appeared: and then, with one look, one word— And as they all stood in horror and amazement, I'd slip out, back to the woods, back to Branty, gallop home, and say to Canoc, "You were afraid to go kill him, so I did it."

But I did not do it. I believed the story as I told it to myself, but not when it was over.

I told it to myself so often that I wore it out, and then I had no story to tell at all.

I went far into the dark, that year.

Somewhere in the dark at last I turned around, not knowing I was doing so. It was Chaos, there was no forward and back, no direction; but I turned, and the way I went then was back, towards the light. Coaly was my companion in the dark and the silence. Gry was my guide on the way back.

She came once when I was sitting in the hearth seat. There was no fire, it was May or June, and only the kitchen fire was lighted; but the hearth seat was where

I sat most of the day, most days. I heard her come, the light clatter of Star's hoofs in the courtyard, Gry's voice, Sosso greeting her and saying, "He's where he always is"—and then her hand on my shoulder; but more, this time; she leaned down and kissed my cheek.

I had not been kissed, I had scarcely been touched, by any human being since my mother's death. The touch ran through my body like lightning through a cloud. I caught my breath with the shock and sweetness of it.

"Ash-Prince," Gry said. She smelled of horse sweat and grass, and her voice was the wind in the leaves. She sat down beside me. "Do you remember that?"

I shook my head.

"Oh, you must. You remember all the stories. But that one was a long time ago. When we were little."

I still said nothing. The habit of silence is lead on the tongue. She went on, "The Ash-Prince was the boy who slept in the hearth corner because his parents wouldn't let him have a bed—"

"Foster parents."

"That's right. His parents lost him. How do you lose a boy? They must have been very careless."

"They were a king and queen. A witch stole him."

"That's right! He went outdoors to play, and the witch came out of the forest—and she held out a sweet ripe pear—and as soon as he bit into it she said, 'Ah, ha, sticky-chin, you're mine!'" Gry laughed with delight as she recovered this. "So they called him Stickychin! But then what happened?"

"The witch gave him to a poor couple who already had six children and didn't want a seventh. But she paid them with a gold piece to take him in and bring him up." The language, the rhythm of the words, brought the story I had not thought of for ten years straight to my mind, and with it the music of my mother's voice as she told it. "So he became their serf and servant, at their beck and call, and it was, 'Stickychin, do this!' and 'Stickychin, do that!' and never a free moment for him till late at night when all the work was done and he could creep into the hearth corner and sleep in the warm ashes."

I stopped.

"Oh, Orrec, go on," Gry said very low.

So I went on and told the tale of the Ash-Prince, and how he came into his kingdom at last.

When I was done there was a little silence. Gry blew her nose. "Think of crying over a fairy tale," she said. "But it made me think of Melle…Coaly, you have ashy paws. Give me your paw. Yes." Some cleaning operation ensued, and Coaly stood up and shook herself with great vigor. "Let's go out," said Gry, and she too stood up, but I sat still.

"Come see what Star can do," she coaxed.

She said "see," and so did I usually, for it's laborious to find some other, more exact, exclusive word every time; but this time, because something had changed in me, because I had turned around and did not know it, I broke out—"I can't see what Star does. I can't see anything. There's no use in it, Gry. Go on home. It's stupid, you coming here. It's no use."

There was a little pause. Gry said, "I can decide that for myself, Orrec."

"Then do it. Use your head!"

"Use your own. There's nothing wrong with it except that you don't use it any more. Exactly like your eyes!"

At that the rage broke out in me, the old, stifling, smothering rage of frustration I had felt when I tried to use my gift. I reached out for my staff, Blind Caddard's staff, and stood up. "Get out, Gry," I said. "Get out before I hurt you."

"Lift your blindfold, then!"

Goaded to fury, I struck out at her with the staff—blindly. The blow fell on air and darkness.

Coaly gave a sharp, warning bark, and I felt her come up hard against my knees, blocking me from going forward.

I reached down and stroked her head. "It's all right, Coaly," I muttered. I was shaking with stress and shame.

Gry spoke presently from a little distance away. "I'll be in the stable. Roanie hasn't been out for days. I want to look at her legs. We can ride if you want to." And she left.

I rubbed my hands over my face. Both hands and face felt gritty. I was probably smearing ash on my face and hair. I went to the scullery and stuck my head in the water and washed my hands, and then told Coaly to take me to the stable. My legs were still shaky. I felt as I thought a very old man must feel; and Coaly knew it, going slower than usual, taking care of me.

My father and Alloc were out on the stallions. Roanie had the stable to herself and was in the big stall, where the horse could lie down. Coaly led me to her. Gry said, "Feel here. That's the rheumatism." She took my hand and guided it to the horse's foreleg, the hock and powerful, delicate cannon bone up to the knee. I could feel the burning heat in the joints.

"Oh, Roanie," Gry said, softly whacking the old mare, who groaned and leaned up against her as she always did when she was petted or curried.

"I don't know if I should be riding her," I said.

"I don't know. She should have some exercise, though."

"I can walk her out."

"Maybe you should. You've got so much heavier."

It was true. Inactive as I had been for so long, and though food had little taste or savor to it ever since I had put on the blindfold, I was always hungry, and Rab and Sosso and the kitchen girls could feed me if they could do nothing else for me. I had put on weight, and grown taller so fast that my bones ached at night. I was always knocking my head on lintels that hadn't been anywhere near it last year.

I put the lead on Roanie's bridle—I had considerable skill at doing such things by now—and led her out, while Gry took Star to the mounting block and got up on her bareback. So we went out of the courtyard and up the glen path, Coaly leading me and I leading Roanie. I could hear how uneven her steps were behind me. "It's like she's saying *ow, ow, ow*," I said.

"She is," said Gry, riding ahead.

"Can you hear her?"

"If I make the link."

"Can you hear me?"

"No."

"Why not?"

"I can't make the link."

"Why not?"

"Words get in the way. Words and…everything. I can make a link with little tiny babies. That's how we know when a woman's pregnant. We can make a link. But as the baby gets human, it goes out of reach. You can't call, you can't hear."

We went on in silence. The farther we went, the easier it seemed to be for Roanie, so we circled round to the Ashbrook path. I said, "Tell me what it looks like, when we come to that place."

"It hasn't changed much," Gry said when we came past the ruined hillside. "A little more grass. But it's still what's-its-name."

"Chaos. Is the tree still there?"

"Just a snag of it."

We turned back there. I said, "You know, what's strange is that I can't even remember doing that. As if I opened my eyes and it was done."

"But isn't that how your gift works?"

"No. Not with your eyes closed! Why else am I wearing this damned bandage? So I can't do it!"

"But being a wild gift— You didn't mean to do it— And it happened so fast—"

"I suppose so." But I had meant to do it, I thought.

Roanie and I plodded on while the others danced before us.

"Orrec, I'm sorry I said to lift your blindfold."

"I'm sorry I missed you with that staff."

She didn't laugh, but I felt better.

◆ ◆ ◆

IT WAS NOT THAT day, but not very long after, that Gry asked me about the books—meaning what Melle had written in the autumn and winter of her illness. She asked where the books were.

"In the chest in her room." I still jealously thought of it as her room, though it was where Canoc had sat and slept for a year and a half now.

"I wonder if I could read them."

"You're the only person in the Uplands that could," I said with the random bitterness that came into all my words now.

"I don't know. It was always so hard. I can't remember some of the letters now...But you could read them."

"Oh yes. When I take the blindfold off. When pigs fly."

"But listen, Orrec."

"That's the one thing I can do."

"You could try reading. You could try just for a little while, just with one of the books. Not looking at anything else." Gry's voice had gone husky. "You aren't going to destroy everything you look at! If all you look at is what your mother wrote! She wrote it all for you."

Gry did not know that I had seen Melle's face before she died. No one knew that but my father. No one knew what I knew, that I would never have hurt Melle. Would I destroy, now, the one thing she had left me?

I couldn't answer Gry at all.

I had never promised my father not to lift the blindfold. There was no bond of words, but there was a bond, and it held me. Yet it had held me when there was no need for it—it had kept me from seeing my mother all the last year of her life, and made me useless to her, for no reason. Or rather, for the reason that my blindness was useful to my father, making me his weapon, his threat against enemies. But was my loyalty only to him?

I could not get any further than that for a long time. Gry said no more about it, and I thought I had put it out of my head.

But along in the autumn, as we were in the stable together, I rubbing liniment into Roanie's knees and Canoc paring at a hoof that was giving Greylag trouble, I said abruptly, "Father, I want to see those books Mother wrote."

"Books?" he said in a bewildered voice.

"The book she made me a long time ago, and the ones she wrote when she was sick. They're in the chest. In the tower room."

Out of a silence he said, "What good are they to you?"

"I want to have them. She made them for me."

"Take them if you want."

"I will," I said, and Roanie stepped back, because in fighting my anger I had gripped her sore knee too hard. I hated my father. He cared nothing for me, nothing for the work my mother had spent her last energy on, nothing for anything but being Brantor of Caspromant and forcing everybody to do his will.

I finished with the mare, washed my hands, and went straight to the tower room while I knew my father would not be there. Coaly led me eagerly up the stairs, as if she expected to find Melle there. The room was cold and had a desolate feel to it. I blundered about finding the chest, and put my hand out to find the footboard of the bed. The shawl lay folded on it, the brown shawl my grandmother had woven and my mother had worn when she was cold, when she was dying. I knew the feel of it, the rough softness of the homespun wool. I stooped and buried my face in it. But I did not breathe in the scent of my mother, the faint fragrance I remembered. The shawl smelled of sweat and salt.

"To the window, Coaly," I said, and we managed to locate the chest. I raised the lid and felt the sheets of linen canvas stacked inside it. There was much more than I could carry one-handed. I felt down among the stiff pieces until I came to the bound book, the first she had made me, the *History of Lord Raniu*. I took it out and closed the lid. As Coaly led me out of the room I reached out and touched the shawl again, with a queer pinching at my heart that I didn't try to understand.

All I had in mind was to have the book, to have the thing Mother had given me, made for me, left to me. That was enough. So I thought. I put it on the table in my room, where everything had its place and was never out of its place and no one was allowed to touch anything. I went in to supper, and ate in silence with my silent father.

At the end of the meal, he asked, "Did you find the book?" He said the word hesitantly.

I nodded, with a sudden spiteful pleasure, jeering at him in my mind: You don't know what it is, you don't know what to do with it, you can't read!

And when I was alone in my room, I sat at the table for some while, and then deliberately and carefully slipped off the blindfold and took the pads from my eyes.

And saw darkness.

I almost screamed aloud. My heart beat with terror and my head spun, and it was I don't know how long before I realised that somewhere in front of me hung a shape full of tiny blurred silver specks. I was seeing it. It was the window frame, and the stars.

There was, after all, no light in my room. I would have to go to the kitchen to fetch a flint and steel and a lamp or candle. And what would they say in the kitchen if I asked for such things?

As I grew a little more used to seeing, I could make out the whitish oblong of the book on the table in the starlight. I ran my hand over it, and saw the shadowy movement. To make the movement and to see it gave me such pleasure that I did it again and again. I looked up, and saw the autumn stars. I gazed at them long enough that I saw their slow movement to the west. It was enough.

I put the pads back over my eyes and tied the blindfold carefully, and undressed, and got into bed.

I had never thought for a moment, as I looked at the book and my hand, that I might destroy them; the thought of my perilous gift had not entered my mind; it had been filled with the gift of seeing. Because I could see, could I destroy the stars?

✦ 15 ✦

For many days it was enough to have the pages Melle had written for me, which I brought down to my room and kept in a carved box. I read them every morning at first light, waking when the cocks began to crow, getting up to sit at the table with the blindfold round my forehead, ready to pull it down over my eyes should someone enter the room. I was scrupulous not to look anywhere but at the written leaves, and—once at the beginning, once at the end—up at the window, to see the sky. I reasoned that I could do no harm reading my mother's writing and looking up into the light.

I was particularly careful, though it was extremely

difficult, not to look at Coaly. I longed to see her. If she was in the room, I knew I could not keep my eyes from her; and that idea sent a chill through me. I tried to sit with my hands cupped around my eyes so I could see only the writing, but it was not safe. I shut my eyes and shut poor Coaly out of the room. "Stay," I told her outside my door, and I heard her tail give a small, obedient thump. I felt like a traitor when I shut the door.

I was often puzzled to know what I was reading, for the linen pages had been put away in the chest in no order and further confused by my carrying them away; and my mother had written down whatever she could remember as it came into her head, often only bits and passages without beginning or end or anything to explain them. When she first began to write, she had put in notes: "This is from the Worship of Ennu my Grandmother taught me, it is for women to speak," or "I do not know more of this Tale of the Blessed Momu." Several of the pages were headed "For My Son Orrec of Caspromant." One of the earlier ones, a legend about the founding of Derris Water, was titled "Drops from the Bucket of the Well of Melle Aulitta of Derris Water and Caspromant, for My Dear Son." As her illness grew worse, which I could see in the weakness and hastiness of the writing, there were no explanations and more fragments. And instead of stories there were poems and chants, all written out in cramped lines clear across the sheet, so that I only heard the poetry if I spoke it aloud. Some of the later pages were very hard to decipher. The last—it had been the topmost in the trunk, and I had kept it in place—had only a few pale lines written on it. I remembered how she said she was too tired to write any more for a while.

I suppose it seems strange that, after the intense delight of reading these precious gifts my mother left for me, I was willing to close the darkness down on my eyes again and stumble through the day led by a dog. I was not merely willing, I was ready. The only way I could defend Caspromant was by being blind, so I was blind. I had found a redeeming joy to lighten my duty, but it was no less my duty.

I was aware that I hadn't found this redemption for myself. It was Gry who had said, "You could read them." It being autumn, she was busy at Roddmant with the harvest and could seldom come over; but as soon as she did, I took her to my room and showed her the box of writings and told her that I was reading them.

She seemed more distracted or embarrassed than

pleased, and was in a hurry to leave the room. She had a keener sense than I did, of course, of the risk she ran. People of the domains were by no means strict with girls, and nobody in the Uplands saw anything unseemly in young people riding and walking and talking together outdoors or where other people might come; but for a girl of fifteen to go to a boy's bedroom was going too far. Rab and Sosso would have scolded us savagely, and worse, some of the others, the spinning women or the kitchen help, might have gossiped. When this possibility finally dawned upon me, I felt my face turn red. We went outdoors without a word, and weren't easy with each other till we had talked about horses for half an hour.

Then we were able to discuss what I had been reading. I recited one of the chants of Odressel for Gry. It exalted my heart, but she wasn't much impressed. She preferred stories. I couldn't explain to her how the poems I read fascinated me. I tried to work out how they were put together, how this word returned, or this sound or rhyme came back, or the beat wove through the words. All this hung in my mind as I went about the rest of the day in the darkness. I would try to fit words of my own into the patterns I had found, and sometimes it worked. That gave me intense, pure pleasure, a pleasure that endured, returning each time I thought of those words, that pattern, that poem.

Gry was low in spirits that day, and again the next time she came. It was rainy October by then, and we sat in the chimney corner to talk. Rab brought us a plate full of oatcakes and I slowly devoured them while Gry sat mostly silent. At last she said, "Orrec, why do you think we have the gifts?"

"To defend our people with."

"Not mine."

"No; but you can hunt for them, help them get food, train animals to work for them."

"Yes. But your gift. Or Father's. To destroy. To kill."

"There has to be somebody who can do it."

"I know. But did you know…Father can take a splinter out of your finger, or a thorn out of your foot, with the knife gift. So neat and quick, it only bleeds one drop. He just looks, and it's out…And Nanno Corde. She can make people deaf and blind, but did you know she unsealed a deaf boy's ears? He was deaf and dumb, he could only make signs with his mother, but now he can hear enough to learn to talk. She says she did it the same way she'd deafen somebody, only one way goes forward and the other backward."

That was intriguing, and we discussed it a little, but

it didn't mean much to me. It did to Gry. She said, "I wonder if all the gifts are backward."

"What do you mean?"

"Not the calling. You can use it forward or backward. But the knife, or the Cordes' sealing—maybe they're backward. Maybe they were useful for curing people, to begin with. For healing. And then people found out they could be weapons and began to use them that way, and forgot the other way...Even the rein, that the Tibros have, maybe at first it was just a gift of working with people, and then they made it go backward, to make people work for them."

"What about the Morgas?" I asked. "Their gift isn't a weapon."

"No— It's only good for finding out what people are sick with, so you know how to heal them. It doesn't work for making them sick. It only goes forward. That's why the Morgas have to hide out back there where nobody else comes."

"All right. But some of the gifts never went forward. What about the Helvars' cleaning? What about my gift?"

"They could have been healing, to begin with. If there was something wrong inside a person, or an animal, something out of order, like a hard knot—maybe it was a gift of untying it—setting it right, putting it in order."

That had an unexpected ring of probability to me. I knew exactly what she meant. It was like the poetry I made in my head, the tangled confusion of words that fell suddenly into a pattern, a clarity, and you recognised it: that's it, that's right.

"But then why did we stop doing that and only use it to make people's insides into an awful mess?"

"Because there are so many enemies. But maybe also because you can't use the gift both ways. You can't go backward and forward at the same time."

I knew from her voice that she was saying something important to her. It had to do with her use of her own gift, but I wasn't certain what it was.

"Well, if anybody could teach me how to use my gift to do instead of undo, I'd try to learn," I said, not too seriously.

"Would you?" She was serious.

"No," I said. "Not till I'd destroyed Ogge Drum."

She gave a great sigh.

I brought my fist down on the stone of the hearth seat and said, "I will. I will destroy that fat adder, when I can! Why doesn't Canoc? What's he waiting for? For me? He knows I can't—I can't control the gift— *He* can. How can he sit here and not go revenge my mother!"

I had never said this before to Gry, scarcely to myself. I was hot with sudden anger as I spoke. Her reply was cold.

"Do you want your father dead?"

"I want Drum dead!"

"You know Ogge Drum goes about day and night with bodyguards, men with swords and knives, crossbowmen. And his son Sebb has his gift, and Ren Corde serves him, and all his people are on the watch for anyone from Caspromant. Do you want Canoc to go striding in there and be killed?"

"No—"

"You don't think he'd kill from behind—the way *he* did? Sneaking in the dark? You think Canoc would do that?"

"No," I said, and put my head in my hands.

"My father says he's been afraid for two years now that Canoc's going to get on his horse and ride to Drummant to kill Ogge Drum. The way he rode to Dunet. Only alone."

I had nothing to say. I knew why Canoc had not

done so. For the sake of his people who needed his protection. For my sake.

After a long time, Gry said, "Maybe you can't use your gift forward, only backward, but I can use mine forward."

"You're lucky."

"I am," she said. "Though my mother doesn't think so." She got up abruptly and said, "Coaly! Come for a walk."

"What do you mean about your mother?"

"I mean she wants me to go back to Borremant with her for the winter hunts. And if I won't go with her and learn to call to the hunt, she says then I'd better find myself a husband, and soon, because I can't expect the people of Roddmant to support me if I won't use my gift."

"But—what does Ternoc say?"

"Father is troubled and worried and doesn't want me to upset Mother and doesn't understand why I don't want to be a brantor."

I could tell that Coaly was standing, patient, but ready for the promised walk. I got up too, and we went out into the drizzling, windless air.

"Why don't you?" I asked.

"It's all in the story about the ants. —Come on!"
She set off into the rain. Coaly tugged me after her.

It was a disturbing conversation, which I only half
understood. Gry was troubled, but I had no help for
her, and her reference to finding a husband had brought
me up short. Since my eyes had been sealed, we had
said nothing of our pledge made on the rock above the
waterfall. I could not hold her to it. But what need to?
I could dismiss all that. We were fifteen, yes. But there
was no need to rush into anything, no need even to
talk about it. Our understanding was enough. In the
Uplands, strategic betrothals may be made early, but
people seldom marry till they are in their twenties. I
told myself that Parn had been merely threatening Gry.
Yet I felt the threat hung over me as well.

What Gry had said about the gifts made some
sense to me, but seemed mostly mere theory: except for
her own gift, the calling. It went both forward and
backward, she said. If by backward she meant calling
wild beasts to be killed, forward meant working with
domestic animals—horsebreaking, cattle calling, training dogs, curing and healing. Honoring trust, not betraying it. That was how she saw it. If she saw it so,
Parn could not move her. Nothing could move her.

But it was true that training and horsebreaking were thought of as trades that anyone might learn. The gift of the lineage was calling to the hunt. Indeed she could not be a brantor at Roddmant or anywhere else, if she did not use that gift. If—as Parn saw it—she did not honor her gift, but betrayed it.

And I? By not using my gift, by refusing it, not trusting it—was I betraying it?

◆   ◆   ◆

So THE YEAR went on, a dark year, though now each day had that one bright hour at its dawn. It was early winter when the runaway man came to Caspromant.

He had a narrow escape, though he didn't know it, for he came onto our land from the west, down in the sheep pastures where we had met the adder, and Canoc was riding the fence there, as he rode our borders with Drummant and Cordemant whenever he could. He saw the fellow hop over the stone wall and come, as he said, sneaking up the hill. Canoc turned Branty and charged down on him like a falcon on a mouse. "I had my left hand out," he said. "I thought sure he was a sheep thief, or come after the Silver Cow. I don't know what stayed my hand."

Whatever it was, he didn't destroy Emmon then and there, but reined up and demanded who he was and what he was doing. Maybe he'd seen even in that flick of an eye that the man was not one of us, not a cattle thief from Drummant or a sheep thief from the Glens, but a foreigner.

And maybe when he heard how Emmon spoke, that soft Lowland accent, it softened his heart. In any case, he accepted the man's story, that he had wandered up from Danner and was quite lost and was seeking nothing but a cottage where he might spend the night and some work if he could find it. The cold misty rain of December was coming over the hills, and the man had no proper coat, only a scanty jacket and a scarf that amounted to nothing.

Canoc led him to the farmhouse where the old woman and her son looked after the Silver Cow, and said if he liked he could come on up to the Stone House next day, where there might be a bit of work for him to do.

I have not told of the Silver Cow before. She was the single heifer who was left there when Drum's thieves took the other two. She had grown into the most beautiful cow in the Uplands. Alloc and my father brought her up to Roddmant to be bred to Ternoc's great white bull, and people all along the way admired her. In her first breeding, she dropped twin calves, a bull and a heifer, and in her second, twin heifers. The old woman and her son, mindful of their carelessness with her sisters, looked after her as if she were a princess, kept her close in, guarded her with their lives, curried her cream-white coat, fed her the best they had, and sang her praises to all who passed by. She had come to be called the Silver Cow, and the herd Canoc had dreamed of was well started, thanks to her and her sisters' calves. She thrived there where she was, and he took her back there; but as soon as her calves were weaned, he took them up to the high pastures, keeping the herd far from his dangerous borders.

The next day but one, the wanderer from the Lowlands arrived at our Stone House. Hearing Canoc greet him civilly, the people of the house took him in without question, fed him, found him an old cloak to keep warm in, and listened to him talk. Everybody was glad to have somebody new to listen to in winter.

"He talks like our dear Melle," Rab whispered, going teary. I didn't go teary, but I did like to hear his voice.

There was really no work at that time of year that

needed an extra hand to do, but it was the tradition of the Uplands to take in the needy stranger and save his pride with at least the semblance of work—so long as he hadn't given any sign of belonging to a domain you were feuding with, in which case he'd probably be lying dead somewhere out on your borders. It was plain that Emmon knew absolutely nothing about horses, or sheep, or cattle, or farm work of any kind; but anybody can clean harness. He was set to cleaning harness, and he did so, now and then. Saving his pride was not a great problem.

Mostly he sat with me, or with me and Gry, in the corner of the great hearth, while the women spinning over on the other side droned their long, soft songs. I have told how we talked, and what pleasure he brought to us, merely by being from a world where what troubled us so made no sense at all, and none of our grim questions need even be asked.

When we came to the matter of my blindfold, and I told him that my father had sealed my eyes, he was too cautious to ask any further. He knew a bog when he felt it quake, as they say in the Uplands. But he talked to the people of the household, and they told him how Young Orrec's eyes had been sealed because he had the wild gift that might destroy anything and anyone that came before him whether he willed it or not; and they went on and told him, I'm sure, about Blind Caddard, and how Canoc had raided Dunet, and maybe how my mother had died. All that must have tried his disbelief; and yet I can understand how it still could have seemed to him the superstition of ignorant country folk caught in their own fears, scaring themselves with talk of witchery.

Emmon was fond of Gry and me; he was sorry for us and knew how much we valued him for his company; I think he imagined that he could do us good—enlighten us. When he realised that although I'd said my father had sealed my eyes, it was I who kept them blindfolded, he was really shocked. "You do that to yourself?" he said. "But you're mad, Orrec. There's no harm in you. You wouldn't hurt a fly if you stared at it all day!"

He was a man and I a boy, he was a thief and I was honest, he had seen the world and I had not, but I knew evil better than he did. "There's harm in me," I said.

"Well, there's a little harm in the best of us, so best to let it out, admit it, not nurse it and keep it festering in the dark, eh?"

His advice was well meant, but it was both offensive and painful to me. Not wanting to give a harsh answer, I got up, spoke to Coaly, and went outdoors. As I left I heard Emmon say to Gry, "Ah, he could be his father just now!" What she said to him I don't know, but he never tried to advise me about my blindfold again.

Our safest and most fruitful subjects were horse-breaking and storytelling. Emmon didn't know much about horses, but had seen fine ones in the cities of the Lowlands, and he said he'd never seen any trained as ours were, even old Roanie and Greylag, let alone Star. When the weather wasn't too bad we went out, and Gry could show off all the tricks and paces she and Star had worked out together, which I knew only from her descriptions. I heard Emmon's shouts of praise and admiration, and tried to imagine Gry and the filly—but I had never seen the filly. I had never seen Gry as she was now.

Sometimes there was a tone in Emmon's voice as he spoke to Gry that caught my ear; a little added softness, propitiating, almost wheedling. Mostly he spoke to her as a man does to a girl, but sometimes he sounded like a man speaking to a woman.

It didn't get him far. She answered him as a girl,

gruff and plain. She liked Emmon but she didn't think much of him.

When it rained and blew or the snow flurries swept over our hills, we stayed in the chimney corner. Running short of other matters to talk about, since Emmon was such a poor hand at telling us about life in the Lowlands, one day Gry asked me for a story. She liked the hero tales of the *Chamhan*, so I told one of the stories about Hamneda and his friend Omnan. Then, seduced by the eager listening of my audience—for the spinning women had stopped their singing, and some had even stopped their wheels to hear the tale—I went on and spoke a poem from the scriptures of the Temple of Raniu, which my mother had written down. There were gaps in it where her memory had failed, and I had filled them in with my own words, keeping to the complex meter. The language lifted up my heart whenever I read it, and as I spoke it, it possessed me, it sang through me. When I ended, I heard for the first time in my life that silence which is the performer's sweetest reward.

"By all the names," Emmon said in an awed voice.

There was a nice little murmur of admiration from the spinning women.

"How do you know that tale, that song?— Ah, of course, through your mother— But she told you all that? And you remember it?"

"She wrote it down for me," I said, without thinking.

"Wrote it? You can read?— But not with a blindfold on!"

"I can read, but not with a blindfold on."

"What a memory you must have!"

"Memory is a blind man's eyes," I said, with a certain malice, feeling that I was fencing and had best be on the offensive, having nearly dropped my guard.

"And she taught you to read?"

"Gry and me."

"But what have you got to read, up here? I've never seen a book about."

"She wrote out some for us."

"By all the names. Listen, I have a book. It was... given me, down in the city. I hauled it about in my pack all this way, thinking there might be some value to it. Not up here, eh? But to you, maybe. Here, let me get the thing." He soon returned, and put into my hands a small box, no deeper than a finger joint is long. The lid lifted easily. Under it, instead of a hollow space, I felt a surface like silk cloth. Under it were many more cloths, leaves, held at one edge, as in the book my mother had made, fine and thin yet delicately stiff, so that they turned easily. My fingers marveled to touch them. And my eyes yearned to see them, but I handed the book back to Emmon. "Read a little," I said.

"Here, Gry, you read," Emmon said promptly.

I heard Gry turning the leaves. She spelled out a few words, and gave up. "It looks so different from what Melle wrote," she said. "It's small, and black, and more straight up and down, and all the letters look alike."

"It's printed," Emmon said knowledgeably, but when I wanted to know what that meant, he couldn't tell me much. "The priests do it," he said vaguely. "They have these wheels, like a wine press, you know…"

Gry described the book for me: the outside of it was leather, she said, probably calfskin, with a hard shiny finish, stamped round the edges with a scroll design in gold leaf, and on the back, where the leaves joined, was more gold leaf and a word stamped in red, and the edges of the leaves were gilt. "It's very, very beautiful," she said. "It must be a precious thing."

And she gave it back to Emmon, as I knew by his saying, "No: it's for you and Orrec. If you can read it, do. And if you can't, maybe somebody will happen by someday who can, and they'll think you great scholars, eh?" He laughed his merry laugh, and we thanked him, and he put the book back in my hands. I held it. It was indeed a precious thing.

In the earliest, greyest light of morning I saw it, the gold leaf, the red word *Transformations* on the spine; I opened it and saw the paper (which I still took for cloth of incredible fineness), the splendid, bold, large, curling letters of the title page, the small black print thick as ants crawling across every white leaf… Thick as ants. I saw the ant hill by the path above the Ashbrook, the ants crawling in and out about their business, and I struck at them with hand and eye and word and will, and still they crawled on about their business, and I closed my eyes.… I closed my eyes, and opened them. The book lay before me, open. I read a line: *So in his heart in silence he foreswore his vow.* It was poetry, a story in poetry. I turned the pages slowly back to the first one and began to read.

Coaly shifted position at my feet and looked up. I looked down at her. I saw a middle-sized dog with a close, curly, black coat that grew very short and fine on her ears and face, a long nose, a high forehead, clear, intent, dark-brown eyes looking straight up into mine.

In my excitement of anticipation, I had forgotten to put her out of the room before I took off the blindfold.

She stood up, without ceasing to look into my eyes. She was very much taken aback but far too dignified and responsible to show it in any way except by that intense, puzzled, honest stare.

"Coaly," I said in a shaky voice, and put out my hand to her muzzle. She sniffed it. It was me all right.

I knelt down and hugged the dog. We did not go in much for displays of affection, but she pressed her forehead against my chest and kept it there a while.

I said, "Coaly, I will never hurt you."

She knew that. She looked at the door, however, as if to tell me that though this was much pleasanter, she was willing to go and wait outside, since that was the custom.

I said, "Stay," and she lay down beside the chair, and I went back to my book.

✦ 16 ✦

Emmon left soon after that. Though Canoc's hospitality would not permit any lapse in courtesy, it was clear that his welcome was wearing thin. And in fact life in the Stone House in late winter and early spring was thin, with the hens not laying, and the sausages and hams long since eaten, and no beef cattle to slaughter. We lived mostly on oat porridge and dried apples; our one meat and luxury was smoked or fresh trout or salmon-trout caught in the Spate or the Ashbrook. Having heard our talk of the great, wealthy domains of the Carrantages, Emmon maybe thought he'd eat better there. I hope he got there. I hope they did not use their gifts on him.

Before he left he talked seriously with Gry and me, as seriously as such a light-souled, light-fingered man could talk. He told us we should leave the Uplands. "What is there here for you?" he said. "Gry, you won't do as your mother wishes and bring the beasts to the hunters, so you're considered useless. Orrec, you keep that damned bandage on, so you *are* useless, for anything to be done on a farm like this. But if you went down into the Lowlands, Gry, with that mare of yours, and showed off her paces, you'd get a job with any horse breeder or stable you liked. And you, Orrec, the way you remember tales and songs, and the way you make tales and songs of your own, that's a skill of value in all the towns, and in the cities too. People gather to hear tellers and singers, and pay them well, and rich people keep them in their household, to show off with. And if you have to keep your eyes shut all your life, well, some of those poets and singers are blind men. Though if I were you, I'd open my eyes and see what I had within hand's reach." And he laughed.

And so he went off northward on a bright April day, waving a jaunty farewell no doubt, wearing a good warm coat Canoc had given him, and carrying his old pack, in which were a couple of silver spoons from our cabinet, a brooch of jasper and river-gold which had been Rab's great treasure, and the one silver-mounted bridle from our stable gear.

"He never did clean it," Canoc said, but without much rancor. If you take in a thief, you expect to lose something. You don't know what you may gain.

While he was with us all those months, Gry and I had not talked as we used to, in complete frankness. There were matters we hadn't spoken of at all. It had been winter, a time of waiting, a suspension. Now all we had kept back burst out.

I said, "Gry, I've seen Coaly."

Coaly's tail thumped once at her name.

"I forgot to put her out. I looked down and she was there, and she saw me see her. So…since then…I haven't put her out."

Gry thought this over for a long time before she spoke. "So you think…it's safe…?"

"I don't know what I think."

She was silent, pondering.

"I think that when I—when my gift went wrong, when it was out of my control—I'd been trying to use it, my power—trying and trying, and not able to. And it made me angry, and ashamed, and my father kept pushing me and pushing me, so I kept trying, and getting angrier and more ashamed, till it broke out and went wild. So, if I never try to use it, maybe...It might be all right."

Gry pondered this too. "But when you killed the adder— You hadn't been trying to use your gift then, had you?"

"Yes, I had. I worried all the time about it, about not having it. Anyhow, did I kill the adder? Listen, Gry, I've thought about that a thousand times. I struck at it and Alloc did and my father did, all almost at once. And Alloc thought it was me, because I did see it first. And my father—" I paused.

"He wanted it to be you?"

"Maybe."

After a while I said, "Maybe he wanted me to think it was me. To give me confidence. I don't know. But I told him, I said I did what I was supposed to do, but it didn't feel as if I did anything. And I tried to make him tell me what it was like when he used his power, but he couldn't. But listen, you must know it when the power goes through you! You must! I know it when the power comes into me when I'm making a poem. I know what it's like! But if I do as Father taught me, if I try to use that power, use eye and hand and word and will, nothing happens, nothing! I've never felt it then!"

"Even...Even there, by the Ashbrook?"

I hesitated. "I don't know," I said. "I was so angry, with myself, with my father. It was strange. It was like being caught in a storm, in a gust of wind. I tried to strike and nothing happened, but then the wind struck, and I opened my eyes, and my hand was still pointing, and the hillside was all writhing and melting and turning black—and I thought Father was standing there in front of me, where I was pointing, that he was shrinking and shrivelling—but it was the tree. Father was standing behind me."

"The dog," Gry said after a while, in a whisper. "Hamneda."

"I was on Branty, and he spooked when Hamneda came running at him. All I know I did was try to keep on Branty and keep him from rearing. If I looked at the dog, I didn't know it. But Father was on Greylag. Behind me."

I suddenly fell silent.

I put my hands up to my eyes as if to cover them, though they were covered with the blindfold.

Gry said, "It could…" and stopped.

"It could have been Father. Every time."

"But…"

"I knew that. I knew it all along. But I didn't dare

think it. I had to—I had to believe it was me. That I had the gift. That I did those things. That I killed the adder, that I killed the dog, that I can make Chaos. I had to believe it. I have to believe it so other people will believe it, so they'll be afraid of me and keep away from the borders of Caspromant! Isn't that the good of the gift? Isn't that what it's for? Isn't that what it does? Isn't that what a brantor does for his people?"

"Orrec," Gry said, and I stopped.

She asked, low-voiced, "What does Canoc believe?"

"I don't know."

"He believes you have the gift. The wild gift. Even if—"

But I broke in. "Does he? Or did he know it was himself, his gift, his power, and he was just using me, because I didn't have it, didn't have the gift? I couldn't destroy anything, anybody. All I'm good for is being a bogey. A scarecrow. Better keep away from Caspromant! Keep away from Blind Orrec, he'll destroy everything he sees if he doesn't wear a blindfold! But I wouldn't. I don't, Gry. I don't destroy everything I see. I can't! I saw Mother. I saw her when she was dying. I saw her. I didn't hurt her. And the—books— And Coaly—" But I could not go on. The tears I had not cried all through the dark years caught up with me, and I put my head in my arms and wept.

With Coaly on one side of me, pressed against my leg, and Gry on the other, her arm round my shoulders, I cried it out.

◆　◆　◆

WE DID NOT TALK more that day. I was exhausted by my weeping fit. Gry bade me goodbye with a little soft kiss on my hair, and I told Coaly to take me to my room. When I was there, I felt the blindfold, hot and soaking wet, pressing on my eyes. I pulled it off, and the wet pads with it. It was an April afternoon, a golden light I had not seen for three years. I stared dumbly at the light. I lay down on my bed, and closed my eyes, and slipped back into the dark.

Gry came back the next day, about midday. I was standing blindfolded in the doorway letting Coaly have a run, when I heard Star's light hoofs on the stones.

We went back to the kitchen gardens and into the orchard, a good way from the house. We sat on the log of an old tree there that was waiting for the woodsman to saw it up.

"Orrec, do you think that…that you don't have the gift?"

"I know it."

"Then I want to ask you to look at me," Gry said.

It took me a long time to do it, but I lifted my hands at last and untied the blindfold. I looked down at my hands. The light dazzled me for a while. The ground was full of lights and shadows. Everything was bright, moving, shining. I looked up at Gry.

She was tall, with a thin, long, brown face, a wide, thin mouth, and dark eyes under arched eyebrows. The whites of her eyes were very clear. Her hair was shining black, falling loose and heavy. I put out my hands to her, and she took them. I put my face down into her hands. "You are beautiful," I whispered into her hands.

She leaned forward to kiss my hair, and sat up straight again, serious, stern, and tender.

"Orrec," she said, "what are we going to do?"

I said, "I'm going to look at you for a year. Then I'm going to marry you."

She was startled; her head went back and she laughed. "All right!" she said. "All right! But now?"

"What about now?"

"What do we do? If I won't use my gift, and you..."

"Have none to use."

"Then who are we now?"

That I could not answer so easily.

"I have to talk to Father," I said at last.

"Wait a little. My father rode over with me today to see him. Mother came home yesterday from the Glens. She says that Ogge Drum and his older son have made peace with each other, and the younger son's the one he's quarreling with now. And the rumor is that Ogge's planning a foray, maybe to Roddmant or maybe to Caspromant—to get back the white cows that he says Canoc stole from him three years ago. That means, to raid our herd, or yours. Father and I met Alloc, coming. They're all in your north fields now, planning what to do."

"And how do I come into their plans?"

"I don't know."

"What's the good of a scarecrow that doesn't scare the crows?"

But her news, bad as it was, could not darken my heart, not while I could see her, and see the sunlight on the sparse flowers of the old, split-trunked apple trees, and the far brown slopes of the mountain.

"I have to talk to him," I repeated. "Until then, can we go walking?"

We stood up. Coaly stood up and stood with her head a little on one side and a concerned look, asking, "And how do I come into your plans?"

"You walk with us, Coaly," I told her, unhooking her leash. So we walked on up into the glen, along the little rushing stream, and every step was a joy and a delight.

Gry left in time to be back at Roddmant by dark. Canoc did not come home till after dark. Often, when he was out late like this, he stopped at one farmhouse or another of the domain, where they welcomed him and pressed him to eat and talked over the work and worries of the farming with him. I had used to do that sometimes with him, before my eyes were sealed. But these last years, he had gone out always earlier and come home always later, riding farther and working harder than ever, taking too much on himself, wearing himself out. I knew he would be tired, and that after hearing about Ogge Drum he would be in a grimmer mood than ever. But my own mood had turned reckless at last.

Canoc came in and went upstairs without my knowing it, while I was in my room. I had lighted a fire in the hearth, for the evening had turned cold. From it I lighted a candle stolen from the kitchen at my hearth fire, and sat defiantly reading the *Transformations* of Denios.

Realising the household had gone silent and the women had probably left the kitchen, I pulled on my blindfold and asked Coaly to take me to the tower room.

What the poor dog thought of me being blind one moment and seeing the next I don't know, but being a dog she asked only questions that needed a practical answer.

I knocked at the door of the tower room, and getting no reply, I pulled off my blindfold and looked in. An oil lamp on the mantel gave a tiny, smoky light. The hearth was dark and smelled sour, as if it had not been lit for a long time. The room was cold and desolate. Canoc lay fast asleep on the bed, on his back, in his shirtsleeves, having thrown himself down and not moved since. All he had for a blanket was my mother's brown shawl. He had pulled it up across himself, and his hand was clenched in the fringe, on his chest. I felt that pinch at my heart that I had felt when I found the shawl across the footboard. But I could not afford to pity him now. I had a score to settle and no courage to spare.

"Father," I said, and then his name, "Canoc!"

He roused, sat up leaning on his elbow, shaded his eyes from the lamp, stared vaguely at me. "Orrec?"

I came forward so he could see me clearly.

He was nearly stunned with weariness and sleep, and had to blink and rub his eyes and bite his lip to come alive; then he looked up again and said, wonderingly, "Where's your blindfold?"

"I won't hurt you, Father."

"I never thought you would," he said, a little more strongly, though still in that wondering tone.

"You never thought I would? You never were afraid of my wild gift, then?"

He sat up on the side of the bed. He shook his head and rubbed his hair. Finally he looked up at me again. "What is it, Orrec?"

"What it is, Father, is I never had the wild gift. Did I? I never had any gift at all. I never killed that snake, or the dog, or any of it. It was you."

"What are you saying?"

"I'm saying you tricked me into believing I had the gift and couldn't control it, so that you could use me. So you wouldn't have to be ashamed of me because I have no gift, because I shame your lineage, because I'm a calluc's son!"

He was on his feet then, but he said nothing, staring at me in bewilderment.

"If I had the gift, don't you think I'd use it now?

Don't you think I'd show you the great things I can do, the things I can kill? But I don't have it. You didn't give it to me. All you gave me, all you ever gave me, was three years of blindness!"

"A calluc's son?" he whispered, incredulous.

"Do you think I didn't love her? But you didn't let me see her—that whole year—only once—while she was dying— Because you had to keep up your lie, your trick, your cheat!"

"I never lied to you," he said. "I thought—" He stopped. He was still too surprised, too appalled, for anger.

"There at the Ashbrook—you believe I did that?"

"Yes," he said. "I have no power such as that."

"You do! You know it! You drew that line through the ash grove. You destroyed men at Dunet. You have the gift, you have the gift of unmaking! I don't. I never did. You tricked me. Maybe you tricked yourself because you couldn't stand it that your son wasn't what you wanted. I don't know. I don't care. I know you can't use me any longer. My eyes or my blindness. They're not yours, they're mine. I won't let your lies cheat me any more. I won't let your shame shame me any more. Find yourself another son, since this one's not good enough."

"Orrec," he said, like a man hit in the wind.

"Here," I said, and tossed the blindfold onto the floor in front of him. I slammed the door, and ran down the turning stairs. Utterly bewildered, Coaly chased after me, barking her sharp, warning bark. She caught up with me at the foot of the staircase and took the hem of my kilt in her teeth. I put my hand on her back and worked it in the soft fur to calm her. She growled once. She came along with me back to my room. When we got there and I shut the door, she lay down in front of it. I don't know whether she was guarding me from whoever might enter, or preventing me from going out again.

I built up the fire a little, relighted my candle, and sat down at the table. The book lay open, the book of the great poet, the treasure of joy and solace. But I could not read it. I had my eyes back, but what was I to do with them? What good were they, what good was I? *Who are we now?* Gry had asked. If I was not my father's son, who was I?

❖ 17 ❖

Early in the morning I left my room and went into the hall without the blindfold. As I had dreaded they would do, the women cried out and ran from me. Rab did not run away, but stood her ground, saying in a trembling voice, "Orrec, you'll frighten the girls in the kitchen."

"There's nothing to be frightened of," I said. "What are you afraid of? I can't hurt you. Are you afraid of Alloc? He has more of the gift than I do! Tell them all to quiet down and come back."

Just then Canoc came down the tower stair. He looked at us both with bleak eyes.

"He said you needn't fear him, Rab," he said. "You must trust his word, as I do." He spoke laboriously. "Orrec, I was not able to say this to you last night. Ternoc thinks his white herd is in danger from Drummant. I'll be going there today to ride his borders with him."

"I can come," I said.

He stood irresolute, and then with the same bleak look, "As you will."

They gave us bread and cheese in the kitchen, and we stuffed it in our pockets to eat as we went. I had no weapon but Blind Caddard's staff, an unhandy thing to carry on horseback. Canoc tossed me his long hunting dagger, and I hung the staff up in the front hall, where it used to hang, as we went out. He saddled Branty and I Greylag, for Roanie had been out to grass in the home paddock since March. Alloc met us in the courtyard; my father had asked him to stay close to the house, keep watch, and gather all the men he could to aid him in case of an attack. He stared at me but looked hurriedly away and asked nothing about my blindfold.

Canoc and I set out at a good pace to Roddmant, or as good a pace as old Greylag could keep. We said nothing all the way.

I exulted in the powers given back to me. What joy, to sit a horse without fear of falling, to see the bright world swing by at the canter, to wipe from my eyes the tears the wind brought to them. To be riding to guard a friend's domain, riding, maybe, into danger, like a man. To be riding beside a man I knew to be brave, as brave as a man can be, whatever else he was. He sat upright and easy on the beautiful red horse, looking straight ahead.

We rode down to the southwest border of Roddmant, meeting Ternoc near the border of our domains. He had been there since before daylight. Last night a farmer's boy had brought him word, passed from one serf or farmer to the next, that a party of horsemen was coming through Geremant in our direction, along what they called the forest path.

He, and the men with him, looked at me, and like Alloc, asked no question. No doubt they thought or hoped I had learned to use my gift.

"Maybe old Erroy will see the Drums trespassing and twist 'em into corkscrews," said Ternoc with heavy humor. Canoc did not answer. Alert yet distant, as if some vision occupied him, he spoke only to confirm Ternoc's directions.

There were eight of us in all, and four more men were hoped for from our border farms. Ternoc's plan was that we should spread out no farther than hailing distance and keep watch. At the points likeliest for Drum's men to enter, Ternoc and Canoc would stand guard. Those of us who had for arms only a knife or a boar lance would flank them, and our two men with longbows took the end stations.

So we spread out over the grassy, boggy hollows and little hillocks along the edge of the straggling woods. I had one of Ternoc's farmers on my left and Canoc on my right. We were to keep one another in sight, which was easy for me, since I was on one of the hillocks and had a good view to both sides and into the woods. Often I could see Ternoc, too, on the rising ground beyond Canoc. The sun was well up now, though the day was grey and cold. A spatter of rain ran across the hills every now and then. I got off Greylag to let him rest and graze, and stood watching south, west, north. Watching! using my eyes! being of use, not a useless lump in a blindfold led about by a girl and a dog! What if I had no gift? I had my eyesight, and my anger, and a knife.

The hours went on. I ate the last of my bread and cheese, and wished I had brought twice as much. Three times as much.

The hours went on, and I felt sleepy and foolish, standing on a hill by an old horse, waiting for nothing.

The hours went on. The sun was halfway down to the hills. I walked to and fro reciting what I could remember of the opening stanzas of the *Transformations*, and religious poems my mother had copied out, and wishing I had anything, anything to eat.

The little black-coated figure down in the bottomland to my left, the farmer, had sat down on a tussock of grass and his horse was grazing. The little black-coated figure down at the wood's edge to my right, my father, was on his tall red horse, walking him up and down, into the wood and out of it. I saw some other little figures move towards him among the trees, people on foot. I stared at them and blinked and shouted out at the top of my voice, "Canoc! Ahead of you!"

I ran to Greylag, startling him so he shied away at first and I couldn't get hold of the reins. I swung up on him awkwardly and headed him down the hill, kicking him into a run.

I had lost sight of Canoc, of the men I had seen—had I seen them? Greylag slipped and stumbled down the hill, which was too steep for him. When we got onto level ground at last, it was bog and mire, and I could see no one ahead of me. I urged the horse towards the trees, and we got onto drier ground at last. I had just realised that Greylag was lame in the left fore-leg when there was a man in front of me among the trees. He had a crossbow and was cranking it, looking to my right. I rode straight at him yelling. The old stallion, not trained for battle, swerved to avoid him, but clumsily, knocking him down with a hind hoof, galloping on into the trees. We passed something on the ground, a man ruined, split open like a melon. We passed another man lying like a heap of rubbish in a black coat. Greylag ran limping out of the woods into the clear again.

I saw my father not far before me. He was swinging Branty around to face the woods again. He held his left hand out and high, and his face was alight with rage and joy. Then his expression changed, and he looked towards me for a moment, whether he saw me or not I do not know; and he bowed forward and slipped from the saddle, sideways and forward. I thought he meant to do this, and did not understand why. Branty stood, as he had been trained. I heard somebody shouting, behind me and to the left, but I was riding to my father. I slid off Greylag and ran to him. He lay near his horse on the boggy grass, a crossbow bolt between his shoulder blades.

Ternoc was there, and others of his men, and one of our people, all coming around us, shouting and talking. Some of them ran off into the woods. Ternoc knelt beside me. He lifted up my father's head a little and said, "Oh, Canoc, Canoc man, oh no you won't do that, no."

I said, "Is Ogge dead?"

"I don't know," Ternoc said, "I don't know." He looked around. "Get somebody to help us here," he said.

The men were still shouting. "It's him, it's him," one of them yelled, running to us. Branty neighed and reared, protesting all this confusion. "The adder, the fat adder, he's burst open, dead, unmade! And his bastard cattle-thief son beside him!"

I got up and went over to Greylag. He stood lame, his weight off the left foreleg. I walked him over to Branty so that I could hold both horses.

"Can we put him on the colt?" I said.

Ternoc looked up at me, still bewildered.

"I want to carry him home," I said. "Can we put him on the colt?"

There was more shouting, and more men coming and going and running, before at last a plank was brought that had served as a footbridge over a brook. They laid Canoc on that, and so carried him up the long hills to Roddmant. They could lay him on his back, for the bolt had gone right through his breast and stood out a foot in front. I walked beside him. His face was calm and steady, and I did not want to close his eyes.

The graveyard of Caspromant is on a hillside south of the Stone House, looking towards the brown slopes of Mount Airn. We buried Canoc there close beside Melle. I put her brown shawl around him before we laid him down. It was not Parn but Gry who led the lament for him.

Mismanaged, like the boar hunt, Ogge's foray had split into two groups; one went astray in Geremant and came out on our borders, where they did nothing but set a barn afire; our farmers drove them off. Ogge and Harba had stayed on the forest path, ten men with them, five of them bowmen. Canoc destroyed Ogge and his son and one of the bowmen. The rest escaped. A

farmer's son of Roddmant pursued them too far into
the woods, where they turned on him; he wounded one
with his boar lance before they brought him down. So
the foray ended with five deaths.

After a time word came from Drummant that
Denno and her son Sebb wanted an end to the feud,
asking Caspromant to send them a white bull calf, as
Canoc had promised, in sign of agreement. They sent
with their messenger a fine roan colt. I rode with the
group that took the white calf to Drummant.

It was strange to see the rooms I had been in but
never seen, the faces I had known only as voices. But
nothing moved me much at that time. I did our business there and returned.

I gave the roan colt to Alloc. I rode Branty now, for
in that rush down the hill Greylag had strained his leg
past repair, and he was out to grass now in the home
paddock with Roanie. I went out to them every day or
so with a panful of oats. They were glad to be together,
and I often found them standing as horses do, close side
by side, nose to flank, their tails twitching the May flies
away. I liked to see them so.

Coaly ran with me whether I was afoot or on horseback, set free of her leash.

After a death it is the custom in the Uplands for

there to be no selling or division of property, no marriages, no great undertakings or changes made, for a half year. Things go on as they were, as nearly as can be, throughout that time, and after that whatever settlements must be made are made. It is not a bad custom. In the matter of making peace with Drummant I had to act; otherwise I did not.

Alloc took my father's place in overseeing the domain, and I took Alloc's place as his assistant. He did not see it so; he thought he was assisting the brantor's son. But he was the one who knew what had to be done and how to do it. I had done nothing for three years, and had been a child before that. Alloc knew the people, the land, the animals. I did not.

Gry did not ride to Caspromant now. I rode to Roddmant two or three times a halfmonth and sat with her and Ternoc, and Parn if she was there. Ternoc would greet me each time with a close, hard embrace, calling me son. He had loved and admired Canoc and grieved for him sorely and tried to put me in his place. Parn was restless and sparing with words as ever. Gry and I seldom spoke to each other alone; she was gentle and taciturn. Now and then we rode out, she on Star and I on Branty, and let our young horses have a run on the hills.

It was a fine summer and a good harvest. Come mid-October the crops were in. I rode to Roddmant and asked if Gry would ride with me. She came out and saddled up her pretty, dancing mare, and we rode up the glen in the golden sunlight.

At the waterfall pool, we let the horses graze on the banks where the grass was still lush and green. We sat on the rocks by the water in the sunlight. The branches of black willows nodded and nodded in the wind of the falling water. The three-note bird was silent.

"It's soon to marry, Gry," I said. "But I don't see what else we can do."

"No," said she, agreeing.

"Do you want to stay here?"

"At Roddmant?"

"Or Caspromant."

After a time she said, "Where else?"

"Well, what I thought is this. There is no brantor of Caspromant. Alloc is the man to manage the domain. He might join it to Roddmant and come under your father's protection. I think that would suit them both. Alloc's to marry Rab next month. They should have the Stone House at Caspromant. Maybe they'll have a son with the gift…"

"If the domains were joined, you could live here with us," Gry said.

"I could."

"Do you want to?"

"Do you want me to?"

She was silent.

"What would we do here?"

"What we do now," she said, after a while.

"Would you be willing to go away?"

It was harder to say aloud than I had expected. It sounded stranger, spoken, than it did thought.

"Away?"

"Into the Lowlands."

She said nothing. She looked out over the dappled, shining water of the pool, looking far past it.

"Emmon took the spoons, but maybe he spoke the truth. What we can do is useless here, but down there, maybe…"

"What we can do," she repeated.

"We each have a gift, Gry."

She glanced at me. She nodded, a deep, slow nod.

"It may be that I also have a grandfather or grand-mother in the city of Derris Water."

She stared at me with wide eyes then. That had

never entered her head. She laughed with surprise. "Why, you do! And you'd walk in, out of the blue, and say, 'Here I am, your grandson the witch!' Oh, Orrec. How strange that is!"

"They might find it so." I took out the little opal that I wore on its chain round my neck and showed it to her. "I have this, though. And all she told me... I'd like to go there."

"Would you?" Her eyes had begun to shine. She thought for a while and said, "You think we could make a living? The way Emmon said? We'd have to."

"Well, we could try."

"If we couldn't, we'd be among strangers, strange people."

That is a great fear among Uplanders: to be among strangers. But where is it not?

"You'll train their colts, I'll tell them poetry. If we don't like them, we can move on. If we don't like them at all, we can come back home."

"We might go as far as the ocean shore," Gry said, looking now very far away through the sunlight and the nodding willows. Then she whistled three notes; and the bird answered.

———

IT WAS IN APRIL that we left, and I will leave our story there, on the south road down through the hills, a young man on a tall red horse, and a young woman on a bright bay mare, and a black dog running before them, and following peacefully along behind them the most beautiful cow in the world. For that was the wedding gift of my domain to me, the Silver Cow. Not a very practical one, it seemed, until Parn reminded us that we would need money and could sell her for a good price in Dunet, where they might still remember the white cattle of Caspromant. "Maybe they'll remember what they gave Canoc, too," I said, and Gry said, "Then they'll know you're the gift's gift."

Also by Ursula le Guin

THE OTHER WIND

The bestselling saga that started with *A Wizard of Earthsea* continues in this triumphant, potent and fantastical tale of magic, love and dragons.

Every night the sorcerer Alder dreams of his wife, who died young and wants so much to return to him that she kissed him across the low stone wall that separates our world from the land of the dead. The dead pull Alder to them, seeking to free themselves through him and invade Earthsea.

In desperation, Alder turns to Sparrowhawk, the former Archmage, and is told to seek out Tenar, Tehanu and the young King Lebannen. With these three and the amber-eyed Irian, a dragon able to take the shape of a woman, Alder journeys to the Immanent Grove on Roke. For the incursion of the dead is not the only danger threatening Earthsea: the dragons are back. And after centuries of peace, they come to claim what they believe is rightfully theirs.

Ursula le Guin

TALES FROM EARTHSEA

'The magic of Earthsea remains as potent, as wise and as necessary as anyone could dream.' Neil Gaiman

Here, collected together for the first time, are five magical tales of Earthsea, the fantastical realm created by a master storyteller that has held readers enthralled for more than three decades.

'The Finder', a novella set a few hundred years before *A Wizard of Earthsea*, when the Archipelago was dark and troubled, reveals how the famous school on Roke was started.

In 'The Bones of the Earth' the wizards who first taught Ged demonstate how humility, if great enough, can rein in an earthquake.

Sometimes wizards can pursue alternative careers – and 'Darkrose and Diamond' is also a delightful story of young courtship.

Return to the time when Ged was Archmage of Earthsea in 'On the High Marsh', a story about the love of power and the power of love.

And 'Dragonfly', showing how a determined woman can break the glass ceiling of male magedom, provides a bridge – a dragon bridge – between *Tehanu* and *The Other Wind*.

This enchanting collection is rounded off with an essay about Earthsea's history, people, languages, literature and magic.